# Vine Entrapment

A Shady Acres Mystery, book 6
(A wedding novella)
By Cynthia Hickey

Copyright © **2017**
**Written by: Cynthia Hickey**
**Published by: Winged Publications**

This book is a work of fiction. Names, characters, places, and incidents are the product of the author's imagination and are used fictitiously. Any resemblance to actual events, locales, or persons, living or dead, is coincidental.

No part of this book may be copied or distributed without the author's consent.

All rights reserved.

ISBN-13: 9798645872083

Dedication: To all my readers who will miss Shelby and the gang as much as I will. God bless!

And to my sister, Darlene, who convinced me to write just one more Shelby mystery.

# 1

*"You* want to have a garden party?" Why did my grandmother insist on making more work for me? I needed to be planning my wedding, not to mention I'd just received my private investigator license and wanted to find something to investigate.

"I thought it might be a good way to get the women of this community together. Form some friendships." Grandma grinned. "Bring back a bit of the good ole days. We'll wear floppy hats and drink from china teacups. Joyce can make us finger sandwiches."

The chef would be thrilled. Not. While

she often made food for the residents outside of the three meals a day, she grumbled about it. Loudly.

"When are you wanting this party?"

"Saturday."

"This Saturday? As in three days from now?"

"Yes, I've already handed the fliers to Sue Ellen to distribute. All we need are tables, umbrellas, food, fine dishes…" she ticked off the items on her fingers. "Your primary job is the floral centerpieces. I've taken care of the rest."

"I grow the flowers, Grandma, not arrange them. And, I have no desire to attend a garden party."

"Fine. Get me the flowers and I'll make the centerpieces." She frowned. "I'm not sure how I'll get it all done on my own. And, you will be there. You're a female member of this community, you know."

Ugh. Yes, I would be there. "Then you should have given me more notice so I could have made time in my schedule." I drained my glass of orange juice and stood. "Most of my rose bushes are blooming. I can get you a variety of color." I planted a kiss on her powdered cheek and headed for the golf cart waiting outside the dining room door.

I drove around the grounds, taking note of roses in red, pink, yellow, white, and every color in-between. Most were ready for pruning. I smiled at the expanse of color and the brick walkway that wound through the bushes. One of my biggest accomplishments was the English-styled rose garden with its scattered ornate iron benches. Heath and I had spent many a spring night cuddled among the roses.

I groaned as I saw Alice quickly approaching.

"Shelby Hart!"

I had the strong urge to pretend I hadn't seen her and drive quickly away from the Shady Acres manager. Instead, I stopped and pasted what I hoped was a pleasant smile on my face. "What's up?"

"This garden party. I know we can count it as this week's activity, but what about the men? They have no social gathering. Some are complaining that it is unfair." She clutched her clipboard to her chest.

"They seriously care?"

"We don't have double standards here." She frowned. "Of course they'll care."

"What would you like me to do?"

"Come up with something."

"In three days?" I needed my fiancé, Heath, the man I was marrying in a month. Maybe he could help. I agreed to do my best and set off to find him.

I found him hunched over his workbench. "I need you."

He grinned. "Best thing I've heard all day."

I explained about Alice wanting something for the men on Saturday. "I'm drawing a blank."

"That's easy. We'll have a competition at the driving range. Any idea what we can use as a prize?"

"A gift card to a sporting goods store?"

"That'll work." He gave me a quick kiss. "The men will be happy, and Alice will be off your back."

I drove away as happy as a dog who'd gotten into the kitchen garbage and hadn't been caught.

Whipping up a flier for the golf tournament was as easy as finding the clipart. I headed to the main office and the receptionist who also happened to be my mother, Sue Ellen. "If I make copies of these will you put them in people's boxes?"

"Sure." She smiled. "Right along with Grandma's fliers, which by the way are gaudy and in bad taste. Still, I expect every woman here to show up. Alice is in a dither trying to find a place in the garden where all the dining tables will fit."

"The flagstone pathway around the fountain. The tables can form a circle." Did I have to do all the thinking around here?

"That's why you should take over." Mom said. She'd been on me for months to try and take over Alice's job. No thank you. I preferred being outside and wearing slouchy, comfortable clothes every day. Tottering around on heels like a drunken giraffe wasn't my style.

"Nope, I'm a PI now." I grinned and headed back outside glad the day's worry was nothing more than where to have a garden party. Too many of my days in the past had been spent solving a murder.

Of course, once I hung my PI shingle, so to speak, I expected people to be knocking down my door to hire me. Which would be a problem since I already had a job. One that let me live on the grounds rent free. I shrugged. I'd worry about that when the time came.

I drove the golf cart to the dining hall, my stomach rumbling. Despite my small size, I was always hungry and the lunch bell was ringing. Shady Acres provided three meals a day, buffet style, for those who wanted. Most people took the offer.

Heath was already seated at our usual table and glanced up with a smile, waving me over. "Chicken salad sandwich and fruit right here waiting for you."

"I don't deserve you." I sat in the chair next to him and planted a kiss on his cheek.

"Did you get Saturday squared away?"

"Yes, fliers made and handed to Mom."

"Which are now in mailboxes," Mom said, taking her seat across from us. She motioned for her boyfriend, Bob Satchett, a poker buddy of mine, to join us. He glanced from his circle of friends, to her, then came our way.

"Good afternoon, folks." He sat down, clearly still uncomfortable that his relationship with my mother was out in the open.

At first, I struggled with it, but now that my father's killer had been identified and put away, I understood it was time for Mom to move on. After all, I was with

Heath, and Grandma was marrying Ted, an ex-police officer, once she set a new date. Her last one was canceled because of a murder.

My eyes widened. Surely she wouldn't want a double wedding with me?

"What's wrong with you?" Grandma, her ever-present glass of wine in hand, took her seat.

"Nothing." I ducked my head. She always knew when I was lying.

"Liar, but I'm too busy to dig into why you aren't being truthful. Ted and I have set our wedding date. It's May 27."

And there it was. "This May?"

"Of course. We'll have matching gowns!"

Heath reached under the table for my hand and gave me a squeeze. "We'll work it out," he whispered, his breath tickling my neck.

I nodded, tears of frustration burning my lids, and stabbed a piece of cantaloupe so hard it skittered off my plate and onto the floor.

"Seriously, Shelby." Grandma shook her head. "I think you're working too hard. It must be all those murders you've solved."

"That's it. Yeah." I picked up the rogue piece of fruit with a napkin and concentrated on eating.

"I was thinking just last night," she said, "on how we've gone a couple of months without a tragedy. Things are getting downright boring."

"Please don't say that." Mom rolled her eyes. "Take up a hobby or something."

"I have one. Solving crime with Shelby."

Lord help us all.

"She's got her license and everything. We're legit now. Long live the Shady Acres Gumshoes." Grandma upped her glass and finished her wine. "Well, I'm off to pick Teddy up from the airport. Don't forget. It's hats and dresses on Saturday. Ciao!"

I watched her leave, then turned to

Mom. "She can't get married the same day as me!"

"Why not? It'll make her happy. She's an old woman."

I turned to my fiancé. "Well?"

He shrugged. "All I care about is marrying you. I won't notice anything else."

While his words were sweet, I wanted to punch him. My first attempt at getting married resulted in the no-good coward ditching me at the altar. I wanted things to be perfect this time around. I had a month to change Grandma's mind.

After lunch, I knelt on a rubber knee pad and pulled vines that had crawled into places they weren't wanted. I tossed them in a bucket as I went, my mind on my wedding. I wanted flowers from this garden, and I wanted the ceremony at the gazebo in the center of the maze near the forest. I wanted twinkling lights as I said "I do" at dusk. And I didn't want to share my day.

Sighing, I got to my feet and wiped the

red Arkansas clay from my bright blue rain boots. Maybe if I told Grandma I wanted to be married in overalls and white rain boots, she'd change her mind about a double wedding.

Yep, a little white lie, so to speak, might work after all. Grinning, I climbed back into the golf cart and sped toward home to formulate a plan I'd call "Wedding Day Shelby's way".

# 2

The day of the garden party dawned clear and warm. The white floppy hat I wore shaded my eyes and a slight breeze teased the hem of my mid-calf floral dress. I felt pretty and had a slight bounce to my step as I made my way to where the tables were set up.

"Why are you grinning like a fat kid with an ice cream cone?" Grandma set out bottles of champagne next to orange juice.

"It's a beautiful day. I thought this was a tea party."

"I said garden party, dear. We're having brunch." She glanced at the round tables covered with starched white tablecloths. "The center pieces are lovely."

I curtsied. "Thank you. I thought pinks and yellows fit the theme."

Grandma turned to greet the arriving guests. "Uh oh."

"What?" I glanced at the women in gaudy hats and flowing dresses.

"Birdie brought Betty Jackson. Nobody likes her. She's not even a resident!" Feathers ruffled, Grandma marched over to Birdie, who had dyed her hair a lavender color to suit the occasion.

The woman with her, Betty Jackson, I assumed, had a haughty expression, Marilyn Monroe blond hair, and wore a vintage style pale yellow dress of a 1940s fashion. Very stylish, but there was an unfriendly look in her eyes as she perused the congregating ladies. I moved closer to hear better. Several women had gathered around Birdie and Betty by the time I got close.

"I thought this was for Shady Acres residents." Aggie Harper, one of our newer residents, glared and crossed her arms over a green blouse the color of pea soup.

"Since when have we not been welcoming?" Birdie glanced around the group. "Seriously! Y'all are like a bunch of magpies, chirping your displeasure. Betty and I ought to just leave."

"Yes, you should!" Hattie Black, our very own queen of rude, shouted. "We don't want her kind here."

What kind was that? I almost raised my hand to ask.

Joyce Rhodes, our chef, and her helper Lori Brown, watched the show with amusement as they filled a rectangular table with finger foods. Where was Alice? She'd know how to break things up.

"What a dramatic performance." Lorraine Hardy, our resident celebrity, upped a mimosa into her mouth. "Who is the poor thing being rejected?"

"I have no idea." But, I really, really, wanted to know. I stepped closer to Grandma and whispered, "What's with all the hoopla?"

"She's a man stealer from way back. Keep Heath far away from her."

Really? The woman had to be in her sixties. Sure, she was attractive, but if I had to worry about someone thirty years older than me taking my man, then he wasn't worth my time to begin with. Uh-oh, Ted strolled by, tossed Grandma a wink, and kept going, but not fast enough for Betty's head not to swivel as if she'd caught scent of prey.

"Stop looking at him right his instant," Grandma said. "I'm not one to sit back and let you take my man and live to tell the tale."

Betty's ruby-red lips curled. "As if you could do anything, you skinny thing."

"I'll show you skinny."

I grabbed Grandma's arm before she could launch herself at the smirking woman. "I think it's time to get the party started. Come on. You're the hostess after all." I turned to Birdie. "I think you should take her away. I'm sorry. Nice to meet you, Betty."

"Hmmph."

My ears burned from the comments hurled after her as Birdie led her away. I would definitely be grilling Grandma later for information.

As everyone filled their plates and champagne flutes, conversation centered around Betty. I had no idea one woman could be so hated. Seems the woman broke up not one or two marriages, but five! Whew. She had been very busy gaining a reputation as a professional mistress. I didn't think such a thing existed.

I ate my vegetables and humus and kept my ears peeled. This was way more fun than a circus.

Mom came bustling to the party and made a beeline for Grandma. "Some floozy is hanging all over Ted."

Grandma's eyes widened and her

mouth fell open. "Betty," she growled. She whirled and stormed away.

I had to admit, she could still move fast on heels. I tossed a mushroom in my mouth and gave chase, along with most of the women at the party. The flagstone walkway rang with the clomping of high heeled shoes and shrill voices.

"What in the world—" We dashed past Alice who immediately fell into step next to me.

"Grandma is on the war path," I said.

"Mercy. Does she have her gun?"

I cut her a sharp sideways glance. "I don't know." I increased my pace to a run.

When we got there, Betty was running a long, sculpted nail down Ted's cheek. She sent a smile Grandma's way, then sashayed down the sidewalk.

"Oh, I'll kill her if she touches him again." Grandma stomped her foot.

"Let's get a lynch party together," someone shouted.

"Hush." I put a calming hand on

Grandma's arm. "She didn't do anything wrong, and people are getting worked up."

"You mark my words, Shelby, she's got her eye on my man."

"Darling." Ted put his arm around Grandma. "My heart belongs to you. Now, go enjoy your party and don't worry about a thing. I've some golf balls to hit."

"Are you sure?" Grandma stared into his face.

"I'm sure." He tweaked her nose.

Grinning, Grandma turned to the rest of us. "Let's go party!"

With cheers, the women all trooped back to the fountain area. Mom and I hung behind.

"What just happened?" I asked.

Mom shrugged. "Your grandmother had a meltdown?"

"Hmm." I linked my arm with hers. "Let's go act like ladies."

She mumbled something that sounded like "We'll be the only two proper ladies there".

The rest of the party went well, everyone on their best behavior, even welcoming Birdie back since she came alone. We toasted with mimosas, told ribald jokes, and acted very much like wild and crazy ladies, then prim and proper. All in all, it was a good day.

I set the last empty fluted glass into a plastic tub and started folding tablecloths. "This was a load of fun, Grandma. Great idea."

"If only the female piranha hadn't have shown up." She glanced over my shoulder. "Finish up here, would you? I've some business to take care of."

I looked where her gaze had landed, but didn't see anything. "Okay, we're almost finished." Monthly social events were part of my job and that usually meant cleaning up, too.

When I'd finished over an hour later, I headed to my cottage and changed into a pair of denim capris and a simple bright pink tee-shirt. Then, slipping my feet into black rainboots with pink polka dots, I marched to finish the ridding my garden of weeds and overgrown vines.

"Hey, gorgeous!" Heath jogged to my side and slid into the passenger seat of the golf cart. "Care to give me a ride?"

I laughed and climbed into the driver's seat. "Where to, handsome?"

"The storage shed. Alice wants me to find an end table for one of the upstairs apartments."

"The shed it is." I turned the key and drove at a ripping ten miles per hour to where Heath stored the community's extra furniture.

"Come on in," he said when we stopped. "Let's kiss."

My heart rate increased. What girl in her right mind would say no to such an invitation? "You're on." We leaped out and raced to the shed.

Heath shoved open the door, and halted. "I could have sworn I locked this."

"You did. Look." I pointed to where

the lock lay, cut in two, on the ground. "Better go see what's missing."

We stepped inside and he reached over our heads to pull the chain that turned on the light.

Hanging from a crossbeam was Betty Jackson twirling like a macabre pinata. A toppled over box lay at her feet. Pouring out of the box were the vines I'd pulled that morning. A few were draped around her neck like garland.

"Why would she hang herself in my shed?" Heath's eyes narrowed.

"I don't think she did." I pointed to the bullet hole in her chest. "She was dead before she was strung up.

# 3

I couldn't believe it. How many deaths could happen at a retirement community? Maybe I was plain bad luck. They hadn't had any problems of this sort before I started working there. I sat on a plastic lawn chair outside the shed while Heath called the police.

When he'd finished, Heath pulled up a chair and sat next to me. "Who is she?"

"A very disliked woman." I told him of the fiasco at the garden party. "If I had to give a suspect's name, I'd have to name half the women in this community."

He exhaled sharply and put his arm around my shoulder, pulling me closer so

I could rest my head on him. "Why do these things keep happening to you?"

"I have no idea. I guess God has a sense of humor in regards to me."

We sat in silence until Seth and an older officer who wore mirrored sunglasses arrived, followed by a bevy of older women clearly interested in why the police were here. Seth turned and said something to them, they paused, but continued following as soon as he started moving again.

"You didn't touch anything, did you, Shelby?" Seth asked, his gaze cutting into mine.

"Nope." I glanced around him. "New partner?"

"Temporary. Wayman is on vacation. This is Officer Glassman." From Seth's stony look, he wasn't happy about the new partnership. "Officer Glassman, this is Shelby Hart and Heath McLeroy."

"So, you're the woman who keeps finding dead bodies and interfering in police investigations," Officer Glassman said. "Not a very fun hobby." He stepped into the shed.

It wasn't my fault. I tried to stay of things, I really did, but something always pulled me in.

"You know Ida threatened to kill her," Aggie Harper said.

"It was said in passing!" Grandma scowled.

"Lots of women here wanted Betty dead," someone else shouted.

Seth's face grew redder by the minute. "Please stand over there and we'll speak to you one at a time."

"Who's Ida Grayson?" Officer Glassman stepped from the shed.

"I am." Grandma stepped forward. "I did not kill that woman."

"Do you own a gun?"

"Yes…"

"Do you wear…" he bent over and sniffed her, giving me a glimpse of a small paper bag in his hand. He'd found evidence of something. "Ida Grayson, I'm arresting you on suspicion of murder.

Turn around, please."

Grandma whirled toward me. "Clear my name, Shelby." She turned around and let him cuff her. "And call Teddy to bail me out."

I jumped to my feet. "Seth, stop him. You know Grandma wouldn't kill anyone."

"I'll talk to him when I've finished interviewing…all these people."

"Heath?"

"Already on it, babe." He punched a number into his phone. "Teddy and a lawyer."

"Let's go to the station." I grabbed his hand.

"Not until I'm finished here," Seth said, stopping me with a glare. "You know the drill. I have to ask you questions."

"Ask me later."

"Shelby Hart, sit down."

I huffed and sat back in the plastic chair. "Seth is mean."

"He's just doing his job." Heath took

back the hand I'd pulled away. "Ida isn't going anywhere."

That's what I was afraid of. They might have enough evidence to keep her until we found the real killer. What had Officer Glassman found in the shed that caused him to arrest Grandma? Why sniff her perfume? She couldn't be the only sixty-year-old woman to wear Chanel No. 5.

"This has to be the fastest yet," Heath said, leaning his chair back on two legs until the shed held him up.

"For what?"

"To get involved."

My mouth fell open. "I have to clear her name."

"I know." He sighed. "I hope finding dead people stops after we get married."

So did I.

By the time Seth finished interviewing those who had followed him to the crime scene, his notepad held several filled pages of statements. The medical examiner finally arrived and shooed

Heath and I to the side out of his way.

"Can we go now?" I asked Seth.

"I need to interview the two of you, then you're free to leave." He flipped to a fresh page in his notebook. "Heath, you first. What happened?"

"We came to get an end table. The lock had been cut off. We stepped inside and saw...Betty?" he glanced at me for confirmation. When I nodded, he continued, "hanging there with vines all around her."

"I'd picked those vines earlier today," I injected. "But I didn't put them in the shed. I left them out to throw away."

Heath nodded. "We thought at first she'd hung herself, but then Shelby noticed the gunshot wound in her chest."

"These are all pieces of evidence no one else knows about, right?" I asked. "That means, when questioned, Grandma won't have a clue and can be released. If not, I have my PI license now—"

"Heaven help us," Seth interrupted. "Ida is only a person of interest at this time. She'll be released. Officer Glassman gets arrest happy…a lot."

There was a story there, one I didn't have time to dig into. "That's about it. Heath didn't leave anything out. After finding Betty, we came outside and called you."

"Did you hear Ida threaten to kill Betty?" His eyes narrowed.

"Yes, but no one liked her. They actually made her leave the garden party. Then, Grandma saw her flirting with Teddy—" Ooops, I was going to suck at private investigating. I groaned. "They had words. But someone else suggested a lynch party."

"Who?"

"I couldn't tell. Too many women were yelling at the same time."

He closed his pad. "Now, you can go."

I grabbed Heath's hand and dragged him to the parking lot. "Hurry. She's been there for three hours."

"Relax, Shelby. She's been there before."

"But I was with her!" I dashed to the passenger side of his truck and climbed in.

"Ida is tough. She'll be fine."

Heath drove a bit over the speed limit and parked in front of our small police station within fifteen minutes. Without waiting for him, I shoved open the truck door and raced inside the building. "Where's Ida Grayson?"

"Hello, Shelby." Grandma waltzed down a small hallway, a doughnut in one hand and a cup of coffee in the other.

"Why aren't you in jail?"

"Oh, Mr. Glassman and Teddy are friends from way back. Want one?" She held out a sugar-glazed doughnut. "They aren't exactly fresh, but—"

"If you aren't locked up, why aren't you home?" I planted my hands on my hips. "I was worried to death."

"About what? Cooperville isn't exactly sin city. It isn't like some big woman was going to make me her girlfriend."

Gross. "Can you come home?"

"Let me check." She yelled down the hall, "Duke? I'm leaving, okay?"

He stepped out of his office. "Alright, but remember...don't leave town. Tell Ted I said hello."

"I will. Shelby and I will also let you know when we dig up pertinent information." She grinned, linked one arm in Heath's and the other in mine, then pulled us toward the door. "Hurry," she hissed, "before he changes his mind. That man has no sense of humor."

Once we got in the truck, she let me sit in the middle, she continued, "It wasn't until I mentioned Teddy's name that he even loosened up. I explained what happened between me and Betty, but he wasn't convinced. I sure hope Seth sets him straight. Me, a killer? Seriously! Now, I know I'm your partner, but I'm hiring you to clear my name, Shelby. I'll pay you by buying us matching wedding dresses. Lots of lace and fringe sounds nice, don't you think?"

Heath hid a laugh behind a cough.

"I want my own wedding, Grandma." I punched Heath in the arm.

"Don't be silly. We'll have so much fun. Maybe we can have a double honeymoon, too."

Heath's eyes widened.

"Ha, how do you like that?" I raised my eyebrows at him. "Maybe we should also share a cottage by the sea? All four of us?"

He shook his head.

"Now, you're talking, sweetie! Get me home, Heath. I have a bottle of wine with my name on it."

I crossed my arms and bounced against the seat back. Not only did a have a wedding to plan and a killer to find, but I had to find a way of having a single wedding without hurting Grandma's feelings. Maybe I could enlist Ted's help.

Mom met us in the parking lot. "Where have you all been? No one is answering their cell phones. I've been worried out of my mind."

"Darling!" Grandma put a hand around

Mom's waist. "Come with me and I'll explain everything. I've had quite the day. Where's Teddy?"

"That's why I've been trying to call you. His car broke down five miles out of town. He's as worried as I am that you couldn't be reached."

"I'll go get him." Heath jogged back to his truck, blew me a kiss, and backed from the parking spot, leaving me to follow Mom and Grandma to Grandma's cottage.

"I hope you have food," I said. "My stomach is growling. We missed supper."

"I've popcorn."

That was all? I was definitely going to starve.

"I've got stuff to make a salad," Mom said. "I'll go get it and meet you at your place."

A salad? Did no one in my family buy meat? I sighed and trudged after Grandma.

"While your mother is gone, let's formulate a plan for catching this killer."

She unlocked her door. "Now, I didn't hold any fondness for Betty Jackson, but I wouldn't kill her. You know that. This is our first case as licensed professionals."

"*We* aren't licensed. I am."

"Don't be such a stick in the mud. I have a nose for crime." She shoved open her door.

Chaos reigned.

# 4

Clothing lay scattered over every stick of furniture, even falling to the floor. Books and magazines had slid from the coffee table. "You've been broken into."

"No, I was trying to figure out what to wear to the garden party and Teddy decided to chase me around the room." She grinned. "We're not too old for a little childish fun."

"There's nowhere to sit and eat."

"The kitchen table is clear." Grandma set her purse on top of a bright red dress hanging over a chair. "I know you're worried about what Sue Ellen will say, but that girl needs to loosen up."

Mom, her arms full of vegetables with which to make a salad, froze in the doorway. "What in God's name happened here?"

"Watch your language," Grandma said. "I haven't gotten around to straightening up. Come in so I can tell you about my day."

"I'm not eating in such disarray. I'm taking the salad to my place. Come or not, your choice." Mom turned and stormed away.

I glanced at Grandma and shrugged. "I'm following her. I'm starving."

"Very well." She grabbed a bottle of wine, then her purse and followed, slamming the door closed behind us. "See? My daughter is wound too tight."

I shook my head and increased my pace. Mom's cottage was the total opposite of Grandma's. Everything was in its place. I swear a person could eat off her floor. While Grandma's place increased blood pressure, Mom's helped a person relax. I took a deep breath of something rosy and headed for the tiny kitchen. "How can I help?"

"You can cut up the tomatoes. Mom, you can set out the dishes."

"Perfect," she said. "Where are the wine glasses?"

"Above the fridge."

"What?!" Grandma's eyes widened. "That's too far out of reach."

"You're the only one who uses them." Mom focused on ripping up lettuce. A bit too aggressively, if you asked me. "Tell me what happened today."

"Heath and I found Betty Jackson hanging dead in the shed."

"Lord, have mercy."

"And I'm the primary suspect since I threatened to kill her," Grandma said, climbing on top of the counter to reach the wine glasses.

"God help us." Mom took a deep breath and let it out slowly. "I assume you're going to use that new license to try and clear your grandmother's name?"

"I'm right here," Grandma said, crawling to the top of the fridge. "Shelby isn't going to solve this alone. I'm going to help her. It's my hide on the line."

I watched her with trepidation. If she fell, her bird like bones would break. "Not only yours. Half of the women here hated that woman." It wasn't going to be an easy case.

Mom placed the lettuce pieces in a bowl. "Get down from there, Mother. We can talk about this over supper."

Grandma hung her legs over the side of the fridge. "I'm stuck. It's too far to jump."

"Come down on the counter. The same way you climbed up," I said.

"Can't. The fridge is wobbly. I'm sure it's from lack of heavy food."

"Eating healthy is…oh, never mind." Mom put her hands on her hips. "Shelby, call the fire department."

"We can do this." I was not going to call because my grandmother was acting like a two-year-old. "Slide off the fridge to my shoulders." I plastered my back against the appliance. "It's only about a foot."

Grandma put her heels over my shoulders and started lowering herself. "I might slide too fast and we'll both hit the floor."

"Just come on!"

"What in tarnation!" Ted dashed into the kitchen, moved me out of his way, and grabbed Grandma.

"My hero." She grinned and wrapped her arms around his neck, then grabbed her wine glass from the top of the fridge.

"Ida, you're killing me." He set her on her feet. "Now, what's this about you getting arrested?"

Grandma quickly explained what had happened earlier that day, then led Ted to the table. "We're eating rabbit food, but we'll survive."

"Or we can have this." Heath arrived carrying a pizza box.

"I love you!" I grabbed the pizza and

set it on the table. "Salad is much better with pizza."

"No kisses when her stomach is empty." He laughed and sat down.

"Sorry." I gave him a quick hard kiss. "More later."

Soon, we all sat around the table with plates of salad and pizza. I'd never been happier. Everyone I loved, except for my best friend, Cheryl Leroix, were around me. When she found out we had another murder to solve, she'd probably find a substitute for her third-grade class and come join us.

Much to Seth's dismay. The poor guy had a hard time keeping law enforcement and his love life separate when Cheryl was helping me. But us girls sure had fun.

"I'm sure you ladies are determined to solve this latest," Ted said, folding his slice of pizza in half.

"Of course! I hired Shelby," Grandma said. "My good name is in question."

He set his pizza down. "Especially since the bullet is the same caliber as your gun. Where is it, by the way?"

Grandma scrunched up her lips. "I normally carry it in my purse, but took it out the other day to clean it. I…don't know."

He sighed. "If someone took your gun and killed Miss Jackson with it, you're in serious trouble, Ida. I'm not sure even I can get you out of this one. For once I'm in agreement with you ladies. We need to solve this crime before you're arrested for good." He held up a hand when I started to speak. "I know you just got your license, but I'm a retired police officer. I can still get access where you can't."

Fine. He could do things his way, and I'd do things my way. My way had been pretty successful so far. "Okay."

I knew from the slightly narrowed eyes of Heath that my fiancé was suspicious of my easily caving in. I'd have to think of something fast. "I don't like you stepping into a job I was hired to do." There. A bit of opposition.

"By Ida? You really look at her as a

client?" Ted's hand paused on the way to his mouth.

"Yes." I smiled. It wasn't until the words left my mouth that I remembered how Grandma intended to pay me. Ooops. I could possibly have doomed my wedding. My smile faded right quick.

"Oh, pooh, Teddy. I really wanted to get my hands on this one."

*Don't lay it on too thick, Grandma.*

"I think your time would be better spent planning our wedding." He patted her hand and stood, then bent to give her a kiss. "I'll see you in the morning for breakfast."

She grinned, then glanced at Heath as soon as Ted had left. "You should probably go, too."

"What are you up to, Ida?" He set his salad fork down. "You and Shelby are way too agreeable over this."

She lifted her wine glass to her lips. "It's easier to agree with Teddy, then to argue. You should know by now we're going to do what we want."

# 5

I lay in bed the next morning running today's to-do list through my head. Breakfast was first...food always came first. Then, I had some herbs to move from the greenhouse to the garden. After that, I had an appointment at the wedding boutique. Mercy. I put a hand over my heart. I was getting married. I had my final fitting today. Grandma wouldn't take it too well when I refused to switch from the dress I'd chosen to one she wanted. Then, if I wasn't worn to a frazzle, I needed to start nosing around about Betty's death.

I shuffled to the restroom, opened the door, and screamed.

Cheryl screamed from the shower.

"What are you doing here?" I yanked the curtain closed.

"I quit."

I opened the curtain. "What?"

"Privacy, please." She pulled the curtain closed again. "I put in my notice weeks ago. They found my replacement, so I quit."

I closed the toilet lid and sat. "What are you going to do now?"

She turned on the faucet to the shower and raised her voice. "I'm not sure. For now, I'm going to help you with your wedding and your new mystery."

"Good. You can help me get my grandmother to have her own wedding separate from mine. When did you arrive?"

"Late last night." She poked her head around the curtain. "You were asleep so I made up the bed in the guestroom without you." She flashed a grin and pulled back.

"Well, hurry up in there. I need to shower. Lots to do today." I moved to the kitchen to start coffee, not sure how to respond to Cheryl's news. Yes, I'd quit teaching when I'd been dumped at the altar by my fiancé, the school's principal, but this was different. My best friend had no reason other than boredom.

Coffee in hand, I sat on the sofa and propped my bare feet on the coffee table. What did Seth think about her quitting? What would Mom say? Cheryl rented Mom's house now that she lived here at Shady Acres. No job meant no rent money.

"I can tell you're worrying," Cheryl said, heading for the coffee pot. "Stop it. Things will be fine."

"How can you not have a job?"

"Same as you. I just don't." She sat next to me. "You found one right off, so will I. Seth said the receptionist at the precinct might be quitting. If so, I'll take her job. If not, I'll think of something.

Maybe I can get hired on here as yoga instructor or something."

I spewed coffee. My six-foot buxom blond friend a yoga instructor? The elderly men here already had lustful thoughts. Their hearts would never survive Cheryl in leggings.

She shot me a dirty look and stood. "You'd best get in the shower if you want to clean up before breakfast, Miss Snooty Pants." She marched to her room.

I couldn't help but laugh. I set my cup in the kitchen sink and went to prepare myself for the day. By the time I'd showered and put on a pair of dark denim capris with a bit of bling across the rear, some strappy sandals, and a blue blouse, she was talking to me again.

"I can't wait for you to pick up your wedding dress. No idea why you went with knee length, but it is gorgeous." She slung her purse over her shoulder.

"I'm too small for a lot of dress. I want Heath's focus on me, not the gown." I opened the door, then locked it behind us.

Not everyone at Shady Acres locked their doors. But then, not everyone in Shady Acres had had bad guys breaking in and trying to kill you, either.

"Are you working today?"

"I was going to," I said, "but thought we'd take care of wedding business first. Why take two showers?" After all, the herbs could wait another day without harm.

Mom hurried toward us as we headed for the diningroom. "They've arrested your grandmother. This morning."

"What?" I froze. "Who?"

"That new officer. Ted tried to stop them, but…oh, Shelby, they found the murder weapon. It's your grandmother's gun."

My knees weakened. "Where's Heath and Ted?"

"They've gone to try and bail her out. Ted thinks they'll let her go under his supervision, but…they might not. I can't go with you for your fitting. I need to be here in case Mom calls." Her chin quivered.

I put my arms around her. "I won't be going either. Instead, I'm going to start investigating as soon as I have breakfast."

"Where are you going to look first?"

"Grandma's apartment, then the shed."

Her eyes widened. "The crime scene tape is still across the door."

I glanced at Cheryl and grinned. "Since when has that stopped me?"

"Lord, have mercy." Mom stormed back to the main building. "I'm not eating breakfast," she tossed over her shoulder.

Well, I was. Yes, I was concerned about Grandma's arrest, but not overly so. Ted would make sure she was all right. With him being held in such high esteem in Boonesville, no one would dare cause Grandma undue inconvenience.

After a quick breakfast of oatmeal and toast, I was unlocking the door to Grandma's cottage so Cheryl and I could start our snooping, uh, investigating. "Grandma was so looking forward to helping find Betty's killer."

"Seth will convince the judge to let her out on bail. She'll only be there for a few days. Golly, what a mess."

"She was looking for an outfit to wear." This wasn't going to be easy. "Look for something that might lead us to the fact someone stole her gun." I headed for the master bedroom, leaving Cheryl to sort through the mounds of clothes in the livingroom.

I stood in the doorway of Grandma's room. It was as messy as the front room. The drawer in the nightstand next to the bed was open. Most likely, that was where she kept her gun. I doubt she would have left the drawer open, but I also didn't think it was enough evidence to prove her innocence.

Drat. "I forgot rubber gloves!"

"Here." Cheryl tossed me a pair. "Seriously, girl. If you're going to be a successful PI, you'd better start being prepared. Did you bring your gun? Tazor? I did." She set my large purse inside the door. "Let me know if you start making actual money doing this. You'll need me as your assistant."

I made a face behind her back and snapped the gloves over my hands. Cheryl was right, but I wasn't going to tell her that.

Prepared not to leave fingerprints, although most of the cottage had my prints, I peeked into the drawer. A box of bullets had spilled. Still, not enough evidence, although I was convinced. Grandma wasn't the neatest person, but she did know where everything was and she wouldn't allow bullets to roll around among her lipsticks and hand lotions. But how could I prove it?

Think like a cop, Shelby! I stared at the floor under my feet. I'd read that everyone left DNA everywhere they went. I knew I couldn't find skin cells, but…there, a blondish-grey hair shining against the wood floor. Hmm. There was also a pure black one.

I scrounged in my pink flowered bag and pulled out a small paper bag and tweezers. With the tweezers, I picked up each of the hairs and dropped them inside the bag. I was definitely getting the hang of this investigator thing.

"Shelby, you need to come see this," Cheryl called from the other bedroom.

I set the paper sack in my bag and joined her. "What?"

"Betty had been sending your grandmother threatening letters way before the garden party."

I took the five envelopes from her hand. "This doesn't look good."

"No, it doesn't. Ida has a temper. If she was angry enough, had drank enough wine—"

"Yeah." I sighed. "I need to call Ted." He was our best hope at helping Grandma.

I sat on the edge of her yellow and white chenille bedspread and dialed my phone. "Ted? I need you to come to Grandma's."

"Why?"

"I'd rather not say over the phone."

He groaned. "I'll be there in fifteen minutes." Click.

Despair settled over me heavy enough to push me back onto the mattress. I flung my arms wide and stared at the ceiling. "I don't know where to go from here. If the judge sees those letters, well, there's motive."

"Yep." Cheryl sat next to me and slapped my arm. Not playfully either.

"Ow!"

"Stop moping. You and I both know Ida is crazy, but not crazy enough to kill someone. We can't give up."

"I'm not giving up. Give me two seconds to have a pity party and figure out what to do."

I'd give Seth the sack of hair samples, then question the women residents of Shady Acres. Yes, I knew Grandma didn't kill Betty, but it wasn't going to be easy to prove. How could I get the women together? Not another garden party. I wanted them together so I could eavesdrop on the gossip that would be sure to flow regarding Grandma and Betty. Then, Cheryl and I could question the ones who seemed the most suspicious.

What would get the women together? An opportunity to voice what they thought needed fixing around the community. With this bunch of busybodies, they'd be sure to all come.

"Shelby?" Ted called from the front room.

"Back here." I sat up and thrust the letters at him the moment he stepped into the room.

He flipped through them, his face paling. "This isn't good."

"Understatement of the year. What do we do?"

His shoulders slumped. "We have to turn them in."

"I found some hairs next to where Grandma kept her gun. I know it takes a while for DNA results to come back, but maybe we'll get lucky." I retrieved the bag and handed it to him. "Will Grandma get out on bail?"

"With these letters, I'm not sure." He sighed. "I'll call you later with any news." He turned and left the cottage.

"What do you want to do now?"

"Visit Birdie."

"Why?"

"Because she's the one who brought Betty to Shady Acres which then resulted in Betty's death."

# 6

I knocked on Birdie's door five times before she answered.

"What?" She pulled her robe tighter around her and glared.

"Are you sick?"

"No, not that it's any of your business. I was up late last night."

I glanced at Cheryl, then back at Birdie. "Can we come in and talk to you about Betty?"

"I don't know if you can, but I'll let you in if you can manage." She stepped back and held the door open.

I sighed, realizing I should have said "may I" to this woman, and walked into her cottage. Birdie's style could only be described as minimal. Nothing but the bare essentials. Not even a picture on the wall.

"How long have you lived here?" Cheryl asked.

"Ten years, Miss Nosey. I don't happen to like dusting. Sit down…at the kitchen table. I've coffee on." She bustled to the kitchen, returning with an old-fashioned coffee pot and matching mugs. After pouring us all a cup, she set out sugar and cream, then took her seat. "What do you want to know?"

"Have you heard about my grandmother's arrest?"

Birdie waved an age-spotted hand. "Ida didn't kill Betty. That's the most ridiculous thing I've ever heard. You're the crime solver, Shelby. Solve this one."

On my first day at Shady Acres, Birdie's best friend had been murdered in my greenhouse. Birdie had immediately asked me to solve the case. I hadn't had a clue where to begin, but had forged ahead in the hopes of making a new friend. Now, this woman was asking me to do it again. "Grandma has already hired me."

"I'll pay you, too. How much?"

Since Grandma's offer to pay me by buying matching wedding dresses didn't count, I blurted out, "Two-hundred-dollar retainer, then five hundred when the case is solved."

Birdie laughed. "You don't charge enough."

"I'll make sure to remedy that next time." I scowled and reached for my mug.

"Don't forget to draw up a contract, in case I don't want to pay you."

She was making me seriously rethink doing private investigating as a business. "I'll get it to you tomorrow. Now, you were good friends with Betty?"

"Nobody was good friends with that woman." Birdie crossed her arms. "I only brought her because we were conducting business, she saw all the women trooping to the garden, and wouldn't leave."

"What type of business were you conducting?"

Birdie gave me a 'none of your business' look, but then shrugged. "She's my beauty consultant. Why aren't you writing this down?"

"I'll remember." Behind my back, I motioned for Cheryl to take notes. "She was an Avon lady?"

"Don't be ridiculous. She sold natural beauty products. Feel my skin. Soft as a baby's bottom." She leaned forward. "Go on. Feel it."

I grimace and touched her face. "Wow. Like velvet."

"Yep. No idea who I'll buy my stuff from now." She saddened.

"Let's stay on track," Cheryl said. "Do you have any idea who would have killed Betty?"

"I heard she was strung up. That would take someone strong." She tapped her forefinger against her lips. "No reason a man would want her dead. She, how does one put this delicately?...she put out."

I spewed my coffee, then wiped the dribbles running down my chin on the back of my hand.

"Stop being so dramatic, Shelby." Birdie handed me a napkin. "After we left the farce of a party, we parted ways on the walkway that leads to the maze. Only, she saw Ted and stopped to flirt. That's when Ida caught her caressing his face. I wanted to tell Ida that Ted was already rejecting her advances, but your grandmother was not exactly nice to us."

"No, she wasn't. I'm sorry about that."

"Not your fault. I guess if I had to name names of those who hated Betty the most, those she'd done wrong recently…I'd have to say Aggie Harper, the chef, Joyce, Lorraine Hardy, and…Hattie Black."

I shuddered. Hattie was as rude as Betty seems to have been. "Why these women?"

"It's obvious, isn't it? They all lost a man to Betty at one time or another."

Betty stood. "I've things to do. That should get you started. Besides, I'm not paying you so that I can do all your work for you. See yourselves out." She turned and started walking.

"Birdie?"

She stopped and turned around.

"Did Betty take a man from you?"

Her shoulders squared. "Many years ago. Too long ago for me to care now." She disappeared down the hall.

"Add her name to the suspect list, Cheryl." I cleared the coffee pot and mugs off the table and set them in the sink. "Let's go talk to Joyce."

"I can't see Birdie killing anyone. She's kind of tiny…like a bird."

"People aren't always what they seem. Remember Scott?" Our heels clomped along the sidewalk as we headed for the diningroom. "Dear, sweet, murderous Scott?"

The son of an ex-gang accountant in witness protection, a man I put behind bars, had sent Scott on a personal quest to make sure I died. He was fine until his father was murdered in prison, then I became a target. Yep, you just never could tell about a person.

Since the community was between meals, the diningroom was empty and no one stopped us on our way to the kitchen. I pushed open the double swinging doors. Joyce chopped onions at a kitchen island while her helper, Lori Brown, rolled out dough.

"Hello, Shelby." Joyce smiled. "What can I get for you?"

"Could we talk…privately?"

Joyce motioned for Lori to leave the room. When the younger woman did, she said, "What's up?"

"We're investigating Betty's murder and—"

"You found out that I hated her." She chopped the onion faster. "Hating and killing are not the same thing. You've accused me of murder before, Shelby. This is seriously damaging to our friendship."

"I just don't want to leave any stone unturned. It's not personal."

She slammed the knife down, point first. "I beg to differ!"

I moved back so quick, I stepped on Cheryl's toes. "Sorry…to both of you."

"If I were to murder someone," Joyce said, gripping the handle of her knife again, "this would be my weapon of choice."

"Alrighty then. Sorry to have bothered you." I turned and shoved Cheryl out the door.

"I thought you two were friends." Cheryl frowned.

"I guess there are conditions to our friendship. Like…not accusing her of murder." Which I didn't, not really. An innocent person shouldn't react so strongly to simply being questioned. As much as I disliked the idea, I put Joyce at the top of the suspect list.

"Where to now?" Cheryl wanted to know.

"I need to talk to the biggest gossip in

Shady Acres." Which was Grandma. The only other person I knew who saw everything that went on here was the local vampire, Leroy Manning, a man so intensely allergic to the sun he roamed the vicinity at night. "We pay Leroy a visit."

"That man freaks me out. He's so…white."

"Stop it. You know he can't be in the sun long enough to get color." I led the way to the far side of the community and knocked long and hard on Leroy's door. Being awake at night, left him having to sleep during the day. I hated to wake him, but this was important. Besides, he enjoyed helping me, even if he rarely gave me outright answers to my questions.

Leroy opened the door and grinned. "I was wondering when you were going to come see me. This is a record. Usually, I'm the last resort. Come in. Coffee's on."

"Too late for coffee for me," I said,

"but I'll take some water and answers, if you have them."

"I bet I do." He winked and closed the door. His gaze raked over Cheryl. "You're quite the Amazon."

She nodded.

I rolled my eyes. Such a big girl to be nervous around someone as gentle as Leroy. Yes, his dark hair, pale skin, and irritated eyes were a bit creepy, but he really was harmless. "Stop it."

She took a deep breath and lowered herself slowly into an armchair.

"Leroy, we're looking for a reason someone would've killed Betty Jackson." I accepted the glass of water, with a lemon he offered me.

"Other than it was a game to her to break up marriages?" He handed another glass to Cheryl.

"That's what we keep hearing." I took a sip. "Save me some time and tell me who killed her."

"All I have are suspects." He sat across from me and Cheryl and grinned.

I tilted my head. "Names and motives, please. I'm supposed to be finalizing my wedding plans."

His dark eyes sparkled with mirth. "Our esteemed chef lost her husband to our black widow two years ago. I call Betty a black widow because she kills marriages. Everyone in Shady Acres knows Joyce has a temper. Aggie Harper's husband didn't leave Aggie until after she found out he was seeing Betty on the sly. Seems Mr. Harper thought he could have both of them. Lorraine Hardy is a little bent out of shape every time Betty is around. The two have always been competitors for attention. Then, there's the not-so-friendly, Hattie Black. Didn't matter that her husband was a man of color, Betty doesn't discriminate."

His list was no different than mine. "How do you find out all this backstory?"

"I listen. People don't see me, Shelby. I melt into the shadows like the prince of darkness everyone claims I am."

He's also been known to listen outside

people's windows, but I wasn't going to complain. His information often got me further in my investigation.

Cheryl had remained silent while Leroy talked, but now she gently tapped the pencil on the pad in her lap. "So, Betty likes to take other women's men away but not marry them. Why?" She looked up, her gaze flitting from Leroy to me. "What does she get out of it? She can't be a serial homewrecker, can she?"

Shrugging, I glanced at Leroy. "Any info on that?"

"Her mother had the same bad habit. Poor little Betty never knew her father. Seems Mommy Dearest got a little careless with one of her men."

I'd bet my favorite pair of rainboots that if we found out who Betty's father was, we'd have a link to the killer. Stealing someone's husband was one thing, but the mistress having a child by that same man was a different story. "Thank you, Leroy. As always, you've been a help." I stood and set my cup on the table. "If you find out anything more—"

"Don't worry. I'll let you know. See you at poker tonight?"

I'd completely forgotten. Maybe my poker buddies would have something useful to tell me. "Sure. Let Bob know I won't be the only woman there. Cheryl will be joining us."

He laughed. "Wonderful. Those old men will be too busy staring at her chest to focus on their cards."

~

Cheryl turned down a night of poker to spend time with Seth. I didn't blame her. If Heath wasn't one of the players, I most likely wouldn't be there either. Although she'd grumbled, Joyce made fresh chocolate chip cookies for me to bring. I was forever grateful to her kindness time and time again. I couldn't cook or bake to save my life.

"Cookies!" Bob took the plate and planted a quick kiss on my cheek.

Since solving the questions

surrounding my father's death, I'd come to accept Bob dating my mother. She deserved to be happy and if this gruff, sometimes inappropriate speaking man made her happy...I wouldn't be the one to complain.

"Ready to lose all your money to me?" I grinned, clapped a hand on his shoulder, then made a beeline to my handsome beau.

"Hey, gorgeous." He pulled me close for a quick kiss. "Feeling lucky?"

"I hope so." I could use the funds to pay off my wedding dress.

We sat around a table with six chairs, forked over the cash for chips, and got down to business. It wasn't until the second round that I brought up Betty.

"I was wondering," I said, as I gathered the pot after my first win of the evening. "Did any of you know Betty Jackson?"

The room got silent as the men, except for Heath, cast nervous glances at each other.

"Well?" I narrowed my eyes and crossed my arms. "There's something here, isn't there?"

Harold Ball, Bob's best friend, nodded. "I think every man here over the age of fifty has spent time with Miss Jackson. While I ain't proud of it, I'll admit it. She had me bamboozled for sure. Coming on all sweet and cuddly while she was seeing someone else at the same time. A married man!"

Bob nodded. "That woman always had more than one on her string."

"Do you have names of these married men?" I glanced from on to the other. "We're all friends here and I've been hired to solve her murder, by my grandmother and Birdie."

"Lord, help us all." Ted threw down his cards. "Is Birdie a suspect too?"

"Yes." I lifted my chin. "I bet that's more information than Seth and that arrogant partner of his has discovered."

He grew thoughtful. "Yes, it is, as far as I know. Heath, I hope you're keeping an eye on our girl. You know how trouble follows her."

"Yes, sir, I am. Both eyes as often as I'm able. Cheryl is with her at night, but my guess is Shelby keeps her gun somewhere other than close by. Am I right?"

Busted. I sighed. "I hate that thing."

"It's pretty, it's pink, and it just might save your life."

# 7

Sunday finally brought the opportunity for my dress fitting. As I'd promised, I slipped my gun and Tazor into my purse and hefted it onto my shoulder. They really needed to make guns lighter.

The best thing about the day? Grandma was being released. I was picking her up on the way. Since they didn't have enough evidence…yet, Officer Glassman said…they were letting her go but keeping a sharp eye on her. I rolled my eyes. That man had a lot to learn about the women in my family.

"Let's go!" I yelled back to Cheryl. "We're wasting time I don't have."

"I'm coming." She marched down the short hallway as she twisted her hair into a ponytail. "I really need to stop staying out so late if I'm going to help you."

"How's the prospective job at the station?" I led the way to the front office to get Mom.

"I've got the job. I start in two weeks." She grinned. "I'll also be making as much as I was teaching, minus the bonuses, but hopefully, I'll be happier."

"I don't think you'll find happiness in your job."

"You did."

"No, it's the people around me who make me happy." I opened the door to the reception office.

The desk was empty. She must be in the restroom. I turned the corner. "Mom?"

My mouth dropped open at the sight of Mom in Bob's arms being thoroughly kissed.

"Oh." She pulled back, her face red. "Uh…"

I whirled and headed for the parking lot, tossing over my shoulder. "We'd best hurry if I'm not going to be late."

I knew Mom and Bob were dating, they'd told me, I'd heard their sweet talk, but to catch them in an embrace? I shuddered. That was a bit much for me to see this early in their relationship.

I slid into the driver's seat and watched Mom bustle toward the car. Cheryl strolled along behind her, a big grin on her face. No doubt she knew exactly how I was feeling.

Then, noticing I was in the Volkswagen, stopped. "You know I can't fit in there."

"You can have the front seat," Mom offered, pushing the seat forward and climbing in the back.

"I'll still be squished." Cheryl folded her frame into the passenger seat. "You know, once you and Heath get married and start having kids, you'll need a bigger car."

"Why?" I cut her a sideways glance. "This seats four. I don't plan on a bunch of children."

Mom leaned over the seat. "About back there—"

"It's fine. You're an adult. It just caught me by surprise, that's all." I turned the key in the ignition, then drove toward the police station. I definitely did not want to talk about that kiss.

Grandma was waiting on the front step. When she spotted us, she ran as if being chased. Once she opened the door, she said, "Put a rush on it. That man might change his mind."

"He won't," Mom said. "There's been paperwork."

Grandma cut her a sideways glance. "Paperwork can be shredded, Sue Ellen."

"You aren't that big of a threat, Mother." Mom crossed her arms.

Grandma tapped me on the shoulder, pulling my gaze from the rearview mirror. "What's got her undies in a knot?"

"Shelby caught her and Bob in a heated kiss," Cheryl said, still grinning.

"Oh, finally." Grandma plopped back. "About time my daughter loosened up."

"Please. Can we just go get Shelby's fitting?" Mom shook her head and stared out the window.

Smiling, I drove onto the highway and toward Little Rock. Grandma was right. Bob was good for my mother. It was time for me to stop acting like a child regarding their relationship.

We found a parking spot near the boutique and made our way inside where dresses of all styles adorned mannequins and filled racks.

I approached the desk. "Shelby Hart. I'm here for my final fitting."

The woman smiled. "I'll get Ganice." She stepped into a curtained alcove, returning moments later. "She'll meet you in room three."

"Thank you." I headed for the room while the rest of my group sat in thick cushioned chairs and imbibed on complimentary mimosas.

In my curtained booth, I stepped out of the dress I'd worn and turned this way and that in the lacy underthings I'd bought to wear under my wedding dress. There wasn't much to them, but the items made me feel pretty.

"Hello." Ganice joined me, hanging my dress on a hook, then removing it from the hangar. "Let's see what else we need to do."

The short strapless gown with a sheer lace wrap over white silk fit me like a glove. "I love it."

"Would you like to see the one Ida bought for you?"

"She bought it?"

"Ordered it online and had it shipped. We're holding on to it so we can reimburse her account. Wait right here." She ducked out, returning with something looking like a feathery tulip. "Do you want to show your family the one you're wearing?"

I shook my head. "No, I want Grandma to think I'm wearing…that until the very last second. If she loves it, she can wear it." Although the thing would swallow her.

I changed into the other gown. While the top wasn't bad, it was strapless and styled like a corset, anything good was ruined by the bell-shaped bottom, worn over a hoop no less, and covered with feathers.

Ganice bit her bottom lip. "Well. No wonder we don't carry that in the store. Mary is helping Ida into hers. The two of you can walk out together."

Oh, goody. I joined Grandma outside our dressing rooms.

Tears shimmered in her eyes. "Oh, Shelby," she said breathlessly. "Don't you feel like a princess?"

"A swan princess, maybe." I lifted the dress above my ankles and led the way outside to the three-way mirror.

"But—" Mom started to speak, but stopped with a shake of my head.

Cheryl burst into laughter and refilled her champagne flute.

Grandma and I took our places on the slowly twirling pedestals.

"I can't believe how beautiful we look. And the dresses fit perfectly," she said.

Not perfectly. The top gaped over my not-so-large chest. Anyone taller than me would be able to see clear to my belly button. I forced a smile, meeting Mom's shocked look in the mirror.

Mary, the clerk who had helped Grandma, clapped her hands. "Only one other person ever ordered this gown, and she never got to wear it."

"Who?" Grandma narrowed her eyes. "I don't want anyone wearing this dress but me and Shelby."

"Betty Jackson." Mary wilted. "She's dead, though, if that's any consolation."

"Get it off of me. I will not wear anything that woman picked out." Grandma tried reaching for the back zipper.

Relief flooded through me like the

mimosas Mom and Cheryl were enjoying. I wouldn't have to wear this after all. "I'll go put the original dress on to show you how beautiful it is." I lifted up the dress and raced to my dressing room as happy as a bee in a sweet-scented blossom.

As Ganice helped me out of the swan dress, I asked, "Did you know Betty?"

She frowned. "Unfortunately, I was the one to help her. I don't like to speak ill of the dead, but that woman was difficult, to say the least. Bless her heart for finally finding a man to marry her."

"Who was the man?" I wiggled out of the dress, rubbing where the wires in the corset had cut into my ribcage.

"No idea. She never did say, and it isn't a requirement to tell us." She hung up the monstrosity and helped me back into my beautiful simplicity. "Although…we need to ask Mary. She's a little nosier than I am and the two were as thick as thieves. Of course, Mary is the manager and Betty insisted on working with her while I hung in the background doing all the work."

I sensed a bit of tension. "Did she, um, interfere in a relationship of yours?"

"Not mine, but she put my sister's through the ringer. Thankfully, they worked things out, with counseling, and are still married." She zipped me up. "Now, go wow your family and I'll see if Mary can talk."

"Now, that's the dress for you." Mom put her hands together and under her chin, her eyes shimmering. "It's gorgeous, but the focus is still on you."

I gave a little twirl. "I have heels for the ceremony, beads and such, but for the reception…"

"No!" Cheryl's eyes widened. "Not the boots!"

"No, silly. I decorated a pair of flat canvas shoes." I twirled again, then headed back to the dressing room. No more alterations were needed, so I could take my fairy dress home.

I joined my family and accepted a flute of mimosa. "I hope you didn't imbibe too much. We do have a mystery to solve."

"Too much?" Cheryl put a hand to her heart. "Moi?"

I chuckled and took a sip.

"You wanted to speak with me?" Mary approached, Grandma trailing behind. "About Betty? Have you caught her killer?"

"No, ma'am, but I have been hired to do so." I dug a business card out of my purse.

Her eyes widened at the sight of my gun. "Oh."

I held out the business card. "May I ask some questions?"

She nodded and gestured for us to follow her to a room in the back of the store. "Have a seat, please. I don't know what I can tell you, but I'll do my best. Betty was a very consistent customer."

"But she'd never been married." I glanced at Grandma, who leaned forward in her chair, her gaze locked on Mary.

"No, but she came close many times." Mary glanced at the ceiling. "Or at least she acted as if she were. She'd put a deposit down on a gown, but never pick it up or pay off the balance. After six months, we always return the gown to the rack. Isn't that strange?"

Very. Betty hadn't been only a serial mistress, but a serial wedding dress shopper. "Do you know the name of the man she was allegedly going to marry before she died?"

She thought for a moment. "Had something to do with dishes, I think."

"Glassman?" Grandma shot to her feet.

"Yes, that's it. Why? Do you know him?"

"More than I'd like to. Let me go find another dress so we can get out of here. Shelby, darling, you may keep the dress you chose. I'm not paying you for this job. I'm partnering with you on it."

# 8

"Glassman was engaged to Betty Jackson?" Heath rubbed his chin. "The man sure doesn't seem like a grieving fiancé."

My sentiments exactly. "I think we need to pay him a visit."

"I agree, but without the others. The worse thing would be to make him feel ganged up on." Heath stood and pushed in his poolside chair to the bistro-style table, then held out his hand to me. "If he gets too angry, he might take it out on Ida."

Again, I agreed. I slipped my hand in his and let him lead me to his truck. "Should we talk to Seth first?"

"Yeah. Why don't you call him and see if he's available?" He opened the passenger side door and helped me inside. After closing it, he jogged to the driver's seat and hopped inside.

I punched Seth's number into my cell phone.

"This is Seth."

"Hey, Shelby, here. Why aren't I on caller ID?"

"Because I don't want to cringe when your number comes up."

"Gosh, how rude." I was tempted to not let him know what Heath and I had planned.

"What do you want? I'm busy."

"Too busy to have Heath and I tell you what I discovered?"

"Nope. Meet me at the coffee shop in ten minutes." Click.

I really didn't know what Cheryl saw in that man. I sighed and slid my phone in my purse. "I'm lucky to have such a nice man as you."

Heath grabbed my hand. "Not as lucky as I am to have you." He raised my hand and kissed it.

At the coffeeshop, Heath's hand on the small of my back, I breathed in the wonderful aroma of brewing coffee. All felt right with my world, until I spotted Seth in the corner, on the phone, an intense look on his face.

"I'll get your favorite," Heath said. "Go calm the beast, but wait for me to tell him about Glassman."

I nodded and headed for a seat across from Seth. "Good afternoon."

He shut off his phone. "Not much good about it. What do you want to tell me?"

"Who was on the phone?"

"Police business."

"Does it have to do with Betty's death?"

"Police business." He crossed his arms.

Heath arrived, handed me my coffee, and sat between Seth and I. "Okay, you can tell him."

Seth cut him a sharp look, then glanced back at me.

"Did you know that Officer Glassman was engaged to Betty Jackson? And did you know that she had ordered a wedding dress…an ugly one…right before she died?" I raised my eyebrows and smiled.

"Where did you get this information?"

"So, you didn't know." My smile widened. "I had my final dress fitting today and women talk. I told you I was going to be good at this investigating thing."

"Hmm." He straightened in his chair. "I don't think my partner is a suspect, but he does warrant questioning."

"We want to be there."

He shook his head. "Not a good idea. He's gunning for Ida big time. It seems she left him a present upon her release."

Oh, no. "What?"

"A photocopy of her butt with a

lipstick mark."

I clapped a hand over my mouth to keep from laughing. "She is creative."

Heath concentrated on his coffee, mouth twitching.

Seth suddenly had a zealous itch on his upper lip. "Not funny."

I shrugged. "It really is. Childish, improper…but funny. Let's go talk to Glassman."

"Nope. I'm talking to him alone." Seth's face hardened.

"I'll just do it another time. Might as well let us be there while you are."

"How do you put up with her, Heath?" Seth shook his head. "She's the most obstinate person I've ever met."

"That's part of her charm." Heath leaned close to me for a kiss.

"Fine, but I do the talking. We'll do this in an unofficial capacity."

I grinned. "Is there any other way?"

He rolled his eyes and marched outside to wait for us. "I'm meeting him for a jog at the track. It might be easier to get him to talk if I wear a wire and you listen in."

"But, what if I think of something to ask him?"

"It's two-way, Shelby." He looked at me as if I were a dunce.

"That should work. Right, Heath?"

"Sounds good to me."

Seth went to his car and pulled out a small black bag. After removing something that looked exactly like ear buds, he put one side into a little box in his pocket, then the others in his ears. "See? He won't know the difference." He handed Heath another box. "You can hear on this."

Wow, technology was great. "You wouldn't be lying to us, would you?"

Heath laughed. "It's genuine. I've seen one before."

We got into our individual vehicles, then Heath and I followed Seth to the jogging trail, staying far enough back to not be spotted in case Glassman waited in the parking lot. He did.

Seth stopped next to a Ford truck,

leaving us to park a few vehicles over. I flipped on the transmitter, putting one earbud in my ear and handing Heath the other. We leaned close so we could both hear.

"Ready to burn?" Seth asked.

"Are you?" Glassman's deep voice came through just fine.

Then, it was nothing more than heavy breathing and pounding footsteps. "This sounds a bit obscene," I said. "Seth, you're supposed to be interrogating him."

He growled.

"Something wrong?" Glassman asked. "Am I going too fast?"

"Man, we haven't even started." Louder foot pounding and breathing.

"Come on, Seth. I have work to do." I tapped my ear piece.

Another growl.

"So, Glassman," Seth said. "I heard the victim was buying a wedding dress before she died."

"So? Lots of women buy wedding dresses."

"I heard it was to marry you."

The foot pounding stopped.

"Who told you that?" Glassman's voice rose.

"Is it true? Because you sure don't seem like you're grieving to me. In fact, you seem rather cold about the whole situation."

"You have no idea what I'm feeling."

"So, it's true." Seth sighed. "Why didn't you say something?"

"Because we broke off the engagement last week. Betty was seeing another man."

"Who?"

"Bill Millow at the other precinct. That's why I transferred."

"This gives you a motive."

"I reckon it does. This run is over." The depression oozed through Glassman's words.

I glanced at Heath, suddenly sad for the grouchy lawman. I knew what it felt like to be cheated on right before a wedding. "Signing off, Seth. Talk to you back at Shady Acres." I removed the ear piece. "Let's go home, Heath. We've heard enough."

"Jilted or not, sweetheart, he could be the killer."

"I know." I rested my head back against the seat. "I'll get over feeling sorry for him the moment he opens his mouth around me."

Back at Shady Acres, the rest of our group waited. From Grandma's pacing, I figured she wasn't too happy to have been left behind.

"Investigating without me?" She planted hands on her hips.

"How do you know Heath and I weren't on a date?" I took his hand.

"Because you rarely go out. You two homebodies prefer sitting around here."

True. I glanced at Ted. "Let's go somewhere private and we'll fill y'all in."

They chose to go to my place. I didn't mind, since that was where Seth would probably come after showering. At least, I hope he cleaned up before he came.

Once everyone was seated around my small cottage, I began. "I'm sure Grandma told you that Betty was engaged to Officer Glassman. Heath and I went to speak with Seth, who questioned Glassman. He told Seth that he broke up with Betty shortly before her death because she was seeing a fellow officer where he worked. That's all we know."

Ted leaned forward. "What's the other officer's name?"

"Bill Millow."

He pursed his lips. "I met him somewhere before. The man was married, but I can't for the life of me remember her name or what she looked like. In fact, I'm not sure I ever met her. I met him in passing at a police luncheon right before I retired. But," he smiled, "I can find out more about him."

"That's my Teddy." Grandma patted his cheek.

"I've seen something in the resident files." Mom's forehead wrinkled in thought. "It will take me a while to go through it all, but I'll try. We might want to get Alice involved. She has more information on the residents than I do."

I hated working with Alice on anything, but Mom had a point. Especially if she thinks she might have seen something that will help us. "I'll ask her."

Seth breezed through the front door, letting it close behind him. "Did you fill them in?"

I nodded.

"I wish you'd stop doing that. Some information needs to remain unknown to the general population." He perched on the arm of Cheryl's chair and caressed her cheek.

"I'd like to solve this mystery before my wedding day. Besides, I'm not telling anyone outside this group. Well, I kind of have to tell Alice."

He whipped around. "What? That woman is a loose cannon."

"But Mom thinks she read something somewhere in the files about Bill Millow.

Alice has access to all of that."

"No. You'll have to find another way."

Great. I'd have to break into her office. Last time I did that, she caught me.

As if he'd read my mind, Seth said, "Don't do anything illegal."

"Of course not." I frowned. I always had a legitimate reason to break into her office. I just needed to come up with one I hadn't used before.

"Let's all go get a pizza," Ted said. "My treat. We spend too much time here."

We all jumped up and were out the door in five minutes.

"Ida is right," Heath said as we followed the others to town. "We don't get out enough. We already act like an old married couple."

My heart threatened to stop. "Is that a bad thing?"

"No, but we don't want to get bored with each other."

I studied his strong profile. Was he getting bored with me?

My stomach rolled. My breathing came in gasps. I was having a heart attack.

"What's wrong?" He pulled the truck to the side of the road. "What's happening?"

"Can't…breathe."

"Forget pizza. I'm taking you to the ER." He spun gravel pulling back onto the highway and rocketed us toward town.

Two hours later I had a doctor who didn't look old enough to be out of college tell me I was suffering from anxiety. Me? Seriously. I was only twenty-eight. Wasn't anxiety something that plagued old people?

~

"Anxiety?" Mom's eyes widened. "I told you investigating murders wasn't good for you." She tucked a sheet up under my chin.

I pulled it down. "That isn't what caused the attack." Tears welled in my eyes. "I think Heath is getting bored with me. Oh, Mom, he's going to leave me just like Donald did."

"Don't be silly. Heath is nothing like Donald." She sat on the edge of the bed. No matter how old someone got, they were never too old to have their mother comfort them.

"But he said as much on the way to pizza. He said we needed to start doing things or we'd get bored with each other. Isn't solving murders exciting enough?"

"But how much does that allow you to get to know each other? You can't have an in-depth conversation when a killer is chasing you."

"I know that, but he's willing to help me. We see each other most every day. I don't know how to make things more interesting around here than solving a murder."

# 9

I pretended not to feel well the next morning in order to avoid seeing Heath. What was I going to say to him? Tears threatened again. I was a sniffling, anxiety-ridden, boring bride-to-be. How could I change who I was so Heath wouldn't leave?

"Stop feeling sorry for yourself and get out of bed." Mom yanked open the bedroom curtains. "Heath brought you lunch. So, if you want him to see you as you are, then stay right there.

"Tell him I'm sick."

"Tell him yourself." She left the room, returning with Heath. "There you go. There's your prize." She left again.

Heath set a tray on the night stand, then sat on the edge of the bed. "I'm thinking the fact you're still in bed is more than anxiety. What's wrong?"

Tears escaped and ran down my face and into my tangled hair. "You're bored with me."

"What?" His eyebrows rose. "No, I'm not."

"You said so yourself yesterday. You said you were bored because we never leave Shady Acres."

"That isn't what I said at all." He took my hand in his, running his thumb across the top. "I said we acted like an old married couple. Is that so bad?"

Was it? Not being one, I didn't know, so I shrugged.

"Well, I can't wait to grow old with you. We'll finish each others' sentences. You'll push me in a wheelchair—"

I laughed and wiped my tears with the

sheet. "Heaven forbid. So, you aren't bored with me?"

"Sweetheart, I can't possibly get bored with you. You get into too much trouble."

I pulled him down for a big kiss. "I don't deserve you."

"I think that's mutual. Now, get dressed, eat, and let's see what Ted found out." He smoothed my hair back from my face and stood. "See you in thirty minutes by the pool. I love you, Shelby. Never forget that."

I sprang from the bed. My legs tangled in the sheets. My face met the floor.

Groaning, I rolled over and put my hands over my bleeding nose. Please, don't let it be broken. Oh, why hadn't God given me the gift of grace, as in lack of clumsiness?

Tears smarting for a reason other than sadness this time, I got to my feet and shuffled to the bathroom. One glance in the mirror and I wished I'd stayed in bed. My curly hair was more of a frizz. My eyes were red and puffy from crying, and now my nose and upper lip were beginning to swell. I wiggled my nose, hissing at the tenderness, but relieved that it wasn't broken. I couldn't believe Mom let Heath see me like this!

I took a quick shower, using plenty of conditioner to smooth out my tangles and being careful not to hit my nose while washing my face. When I was finished, I pulled on a pair of baggy flowered overalls with matching rainboots, a faded tee-shirt, and a floppy hat. I laughed, feeling very much like the old woman Heath had compared me to. I was ready to start the day of weeding flower beds and checking with Ted. Oh, and I needed to talk with Alice.

"Lord have mercy." Mom took a step back when I entered the kitchen, doughnut in my hand. "What happened to your face?"

"I fell out of bed. Is the coffee ready?"

She nodded, obviously choosing not to say anything, and reached for the coffeepot. "Why don't you get one of them K-cup thingies? Then, you can brew one cup at a time."

"Wedding present idea." I tried to wink, but it hurt my cheek, which I must have bruised. "I guess I need to get registered somewhere."

"That would be a smart thing to do." She handed me the cup. "I'm off to work. Will you be all right?"

"Yes, I've work to do."

"Don't let your grandmother see you in that getup. You know how she is about how a lady should dress."

"I'm digging in the dirt today. I'm dressed appropriately." I sighed.

"Make sure to take your weapons." She planted a quick kiss on my cheek and rushed out the door.

I followed, locking the door behind me.

Heath's eyes widened when I arrived poolside. "What happened?"

"I fell out of bed."

He blinked a few times, then laughed. "See? Never boring. What's on your agenda today?"

"Weeding and feeding. I need some fertilizer from the greenhouse. Could you help me? When I've finished, we can go see Ted."

"Sounds good. I have to fix the plumbing in the main building restroom," he said as we strolled toward the greenhouse. "Do you want to meet up in two hours?"

"I should be finished by then." I unlocked the greenhouse door and stepped inside.

The building was my sanctuary. With all the seedlings sprouting above the rich soil, the orchids growing, a slight mist emitting from the overhead sprinklers regularly, I could almost forgot that I'd found a dead body there on my first day.

"The fertilizer is over here." I led him to a back corner and around a high planting bed.

Birdie, gagged and bound to a chair sat there. She started squirming and shrieking.

Heath pulled a pocketknife from his pocket and cut through the zip ties. "What happened?" he asked, removing the dirty rag from her mouth.

I recognized it as one I used to dry my hands after planting. "Who tied you up?"

"I have no idea," she said. "I was snooping in the dumpsters early this morning. You know how I like to find treasures others toss away. Anyway, someone hit me over the head and I woke up here, trussed up like a holiday turkey." Her pink hair quivered with each furious motion of her hands.

"Do you remember seeing anything that might link to Betty's killer?" I pulled up a stool and sat across from her while Heath punched in numbers on his phone.

"Let me think." She put her head back and stared at the glass panes in the ceiling. "I found some magazines I hadn't read yet, a perfectly good pair of shoes that were a size too big…it's all in my flowered bag." She glanced around. "It's gone. Whoever hit me must have taken it."

"Are you sure you didn't leave it somewhere?" Heath asked. "I mean, you were obviously brought here from the dumpsters."

"Oh, yeah." Her face darkened. "Silly me. I bet it's still behind the bush. I stick it there in case someone takes offense to my pilfering. This way, I can pretend I accidentally threw something away." She grinned. "But…back to the task at hand." She tapped her finger against her lips as she thought.

She gasped. "I remember now. I was reaching for a necklace. I swear it belonged to Betty, but the ruby was missing. Betty had told me that the necklace was from her latest sweetie. Anyway, I stuck the necklace in my pocket and started digging for the stone when someone hit me." She felt around in her pockets. "The necklace is gone. I bet the killer took it."

I was thinking the same thing and glanced at Heath. "Is it worth digging in the dumpster?"

"Possibly. I'm texting Seth to meet us there. At least you're dressed to get dirty."

I frowned. These were my favorite overalls.

"Let's go." Birdie got to her feet. "Time only means more garbage." She bustled out of the greenhouse.

With an amused look at Heath, I followed, him taking up the rear.

Birdie led us to a dumpster near the building the workers lived in. I'd assumed it was the resident dumpsters. This didn't look good for Joyce since she was on my suspect list.

"How did you get in? The gate is supposed to be locked to all but staff." Heath pulled a ring of keys off his belt.

Birdie ducked her head. "I cut a hole in the back near the hydrangea bushes. Easy in easy out."

Not only for her, but possibly the killer.

"I'm going to fix the fence, Birdie,"

Heath said, pushing the gate open. "If you cut another hole, I'll cite you for vandalism. Dig in the resident garbage."

"Cite me?" She glanced at me. "Can he do that? He's a civilian."

"He's also the maintenance around here. You're making his job harder." I tried to look stern, but the tiny woman looked so taken aback I couldn't help but smile. Besides, Heath looked angry enough for both us.

"Let's go." Heath led the way to the back and peered around the hydrangeas. "Birdie, I ought to make you pay for this."

"I don't have the money. I'm on a fixed income." She climbed on an overturned milk crate and peered inside the first dumpster. "Here's where I found the necklace."

I stared at the black bags oozing with kitchen waste. No way did I want to get in there. I was bound to get something on my clothes that wouldn't come out. "Go in and look."

"You go in. I hired you, remember?"

I glared. "You haven't paid me the retainer yet."

"Oh." She pulled a check for five-hundred dollars out of her brassiere. "Here."

The check was bit damp, but it would cash. I folded it in the bib pocket of my overalls, grimaced, and fell over the rim of the dumpster. She was right. She had hired me.

"Toss me the bags," Heath said. "It will make it easier to search without so much junk in your way."

"Is this ruby even worth it?" I asked, throwing a bag over the side and sliming my arm with something orange.

"Five thousand dollars is what she told me." Birdie planted her age-spotted hands on skinny hips. "Is it worth digging for now?"

"Absolutely!" I threw another bag with enough force that it broke open on the sidewalk. "Sorry." Finding a treasure of that magnitude making digging through muck worth it, until I came to the realization that we couldn't keep the stone. It belonged to Officer Glassman.

I growled and tossed another bag. When I heard a larger thud than normal and a grunt, I peeked over the rim to see Seth climbing out from under a bag full of left-over spaghetti noodles.

He plucked a noodle off his shirt. A muscle ticked in his jaw.

I ducked down.

"Too late. I know who's in there. Find anything?"

"Not yet. There's a few more bags."

"Throw them out while I question Birdie."

Oh, good. He wasn't going to yell about getting hit with the bag. At least not while I was still tossing them.

I hefted the last bag. Oh! Nestled in the corner…in a puddle of…something brown…winked the ruby.

# 10

"I found it!"

"Let me have it." Seth held out his hand.

"I don't want to touch it." My stomach rolled at the thought. "It's lying in something brown and oozing."

"Chocolate?" Seth shook his head. "Use a piece of paper, then. I've things to do."

Heath peered over the edge of the dumpster. "Yeah, looks like chocolate or gravy. Maybe it's chocolate gravy."

I liked chocolate gravy. I squatted next

to the offending puddle and sniffed. It didn't smell like pooh. So, it couldn't be poop, right? None of our residents wore diapers that I knew of and all seemed to be potty-trained.

I glanced around and picked up a small baggy that looked relatively clean and wrapped it around the ruby. Doing my best not to gag, I held it over the side of the dumpster and dropped it into Seth's hand.

"Gross, Shelby."

"Somebody help me out of here." I held up my arms.

Heath grabbed hold and pulled me over and into his arms. His nose wrinkled and his eyes watered. "Girl, you smell bad."

"There's almost a week's worth of rotted foot and spoiled vegetables in there. I must smell like the inside of a trashcan." I giggled, stepping back. I had been inside a trashcan. What else would I smell like? I must have been giddy from toxic fumes.

"How will you find out if it belongs to Officer Glassman?" I wiped my hands on the cleanest spot I could find on my clothes.

"I'll ask him," Seth said. "He would know whether he gave Betty a necklace and what it looked like. If it isn't his, then I'll try to find the owner."

"If you can't, it becomes mine, right?" Birdie tugged on his sleeve.

"I'm the one who went digging for it." I glared. "I deserve two-thirds."

"Half. You can have half. Take it or leave it." She turned and marched away.

"Mind walking with me to the greenhouse?" Seth asked.

I really wanted a shower, but knowing Seth, he wouldn't want to wait. "Sure. I promise we didn't touch anything except for Birdie."

I walked ahead of the men, gathering quite a crowd as we went. First it was just Cheryl, Grandma, and Ted that fell into step behind us, but soon I felt as if half the community was following.

Speculations flew like bubbles in the wind.

"I bet Shelby is finally going to jail for sticking her nose where it doesn't belong," Hattie said.

"No way," Amber, one of the girls from housekeeping said. "I bet she's helping the cops again."

"Sure she is," Becky, the other maid, added. "That's what she does."

"I think she needs to mind her own business," Aggie Harper injected. "She's a gardener, not a detective."

"That's what you know." Grandma put her two cents in. "She's licensed and everything."

Seth stopped at the edge of the small brickway leading to the greenhouse and faced the crowd. "No one goes past here other than myself, Shelby, Heath, and Birdie. Where is Birdie?"

"She left," Grandma stated. "Said something about being done with the day."

"Go get her, please." A nervous tic

developed near his eye.

Sometimes, I almost felt sorry for him having to deal with us. It rarely lasted long, though, because he'd open his mouth and boss me around.

"Shelby, don't you have everyone's phone number?" His brows lowered. "Call Birdie and call Alice. I'm surprised she hasn't been here getting in the way."

Come to think of it, it was strange that Alice hadn't shown up by now. She usually knew when something big was going down and wanted right in the middle of things.

I dialed Birdie first. "You need to come to the greenhouse. Seth wants to check it out with you there."

"Fine." Click.

I dialed Alice second. She answered on the fourth ring, out of breath, and panting between words.

"This…had…better be…good," she said.

"Where are you?"

"Working."

I cocked my head as if she could see me. "Seriously. What are you doing to make you so breathless?"

"Maybe I'm with a man."

"I need you to be serious. Seth is here because Birdie was tied up in the greenhouse and he's curious as to why the manager of Shady Acres isn't here."

"I take offense that you don't believe I might be with someone."

I sighed. "Are you coming or not?"

"I'm coming." Click.

Why did people have to be so difficult? All I wanted to do was solve Betty's murder, then marry Heath. Was that too much to ask? I was beginning to think so.

Several minutes later, Birdie and Alice came marching down the sidewalk, side-by-side, identical peeved expressions on their faces. Birdie talked a mile a minute, while Alice kept her gaze focused forward. She made a beeline for Seth.

"Well? What have you got?" She lifted her chin. "You pulled me away from something important."

"A man," I snickered.

Grandma snorted. "She was in her office on the computer. I saw her. Unless she was in a chat…oh, my, goodness. Alice is internet dating!"

"I am not." High spots of color appeared on her cheeks.

"Yes, you are." Grandma bent over laughing. "You look as guilty as a kid caught smoking behind the barn."

"Can we please focus?" Seth said. "We are in the middle of a murder investigation."

Heath put two fingers in his mouth and blew a whistle shrill enough to burst eardrums. "No more noise."

"I didn't know you could do that." I glanced up in astonishment.

"Never needed to before." He grinned.

Seth growled and entered the greenhouse. "I'll do this on my own."

I shrugged and followed, Heath doing the same. I glanced back and waved for Birdie to come.

She rolled her eyes and did as commanded. "I don't see why I have to relive the experience. It was horrifying enough the first time." She headed for Seth, rattled off what she'd told us that morning, then turned around. "I could have died. I need a drink and my bed. Goodbye." With those words she cut through the nosy crowd and left.

Seth blinked several times, sighed again, poor guy, and wrote some words on a notepad. "Anything else to add?"

"Not a thing, except I haven't fertilized the garden yet."

His mouth opened, then snapped closed.

"That's not what he meant, sweetheart." Heath hip bumped me. He turned to Seth. "No, Birdie covered it all."

I knew what Seth meant. I only said what I did in hopes he wouldn't keep us too long. I wanted to shower in the worst way, finish my job, and talk to Alice.

"Why was I called?" Alice entered and

glanced around.

"Because you're the manager," Seth explained. "You need to know when these things take place on your property."

She fluttered her eyelashes. "Fine. Birdie seems to be unharmed. I'll fill out a report and sent to corporate."

She wouldn't. Every time something bad happened at Shady Acres, corporate threatened to fire her as if the deaths were her fault. Mom had been on me for months to apply for Alice's job and try to take over.

"Go shower. We're done." Seth slipped his notepad in his pocket. "I'll stop by to see Cheryl later. Ask Ted to come by. I need to talk to him."

Didn't we all? I nodded, squeezed Heath's hand, and ran for my cottage and the shower, calling over my shoulder that I'd see him at supper.

I stayed in the shower until the water ran cold. Even then I could still smell the stench of the dumpster. I dried off and wrapped the towel around my head wondering what Seth wanted to talk to Ted about.

Did he know Ted was trying to dig up information for me? Was Seth also thinking that whoever killed Betty lived at Shady Acres? I was beginning to think under an assumed name. A couple hundred bucks and anyone could change their name to anything they wanted. If I wanted to kill someone and not be discovered through connections, that's what I'd do.

I pulled on a pair of faded denim shorts, a yellow tee-shirt, and a pair of bright blue garden boots with yellow dots. I had a pair of matching garden gloves. It wasn't until I removed the towel and put my wet hair into a ponytail, that I realized I'd left my hat at the dumpster. It was my favorite hat.

After locking my cottage door, I hopped into the golf cart and sped at a remarkable fifteen-miles per hour to the dumpsters. Ah, there it was. Right on the sidewalk where it fell as I climbed over the edge.

I slowed the golf cart, bent over to pick up the hat, and got Tazered. While intense pain filled my body, a sharp squeak erupted from my mouth, a dark shadow fell over me. Then, a computerized voice told me to stay out of the events surrounding Betty's death.

# 11

I tried to will myself to roll over. Nothing moved but my eyeballs, which thankfully, were smashed against the concrete like my nose was. My poor nose. The swelling was never going to go down. I counted to thirty before the tingling left my body.

So, it was a civilian Tazer and not police issued. Not that it mattered, but I was finally able to put some of what I'd learned in a book to use.

"What are you doing?" Joyce squatted next to me.

"Taking a nap." What did it look like I was doing?

"You're a strange bird, Shelby Hart." She grasped my upper arm and hauled me to my feet.

"Someone tazed me while I was getting my hat." I slapped the floppy hat on my head and climbed back into the golf cart. "Why aren't you in the kitchen preparing supper?"

"I needed to get something." She pulled a large knife from a black bag over her shoulder.

"Wicked." I pressed the gas pedal and zoomed away, not wanting her to use the knife on me. She'd had a wicked gleam in her eye that made me question whether we really were friends.

I swiped the back of my hand across my nose. Blood smeared my skin. Great. Wonderful. I probably had a bit of road rash to go with the swelling. I drove back home, cleaned myself up, groaned at my reflection, then grabbed the bag that held my gun and Tazer. When was I going to learn not to leave it at home? When someone succeeded in killing me? Experience had taught me I usually only got one warning before things turned really ugly.

"What in heaven's name?" Mom froze on the sidewalk between the main building and the cottages, her arms full of fliers.

"I fell. Want a ride?"

Not taking her gaze off me, she climbed aboard. "Alice wants these delivered right away. Says we can't put them in the mailboxes. She's calling a community meeting tonight. Oh, she wants to know what you've got planned for the social event for the weekend."

I had nothing, but this did give me the excuse to go nosing around her office. All I had to do was pick a time when I knew she wouldn't be there. "Any ideas?"

"We've never had a hoe down."

"You mean with square dancing?"

She nodded. "Bob used to do the calling for square dancing, back in the day."

"That's a great idea." I knew where I could get bales of hay. We could rent a large tent and decorate it to look like the inside of a barn. A week wasn't a lot of time, but Cheryl was there to help.

"You've blood on your cheek." She pulled a tissue from under her bra strap, licked it, and tried to wipe my face.

"Mom, please. I'm not three."

She shrugged. "Let me off here. I'll walk the length of the cottages and slide these under the doors." She held one out to me. "Here's yours. Meeting tonight at seven in the diningroom." She hopped down and headed for the first cottage.

Time was getting away from me and I still had to weed and fertilize the vegetable garden. I passed Aggie on my way and waved, receiving a glare in return.

By the time supper came, I was hot, sweaty and in need of my third shower of the day. I rushed through cleaning up, tossed on a tee-shirt dress, slipped my feet into flip-flops, and rushed to eat.

Heath waited next to the doors. "I knew you wouldn't miss the chance to eat. I was just about to come and get you. You're never late." He peered closer at my face. "Am I mistaken or are there new scrapes?"

"New scrapes. I'll tell you later." I grabbed his hand and dragged him inside.

"You'll tell me now." He pulled me to a stop.

"I went back to the dumpster to get my hat. Someone tazed me and I fell out of the golf cart. Can we eat now?"

He stared at me without speaking for so long I started shifting from one foot to the other. Finally, he gave a long sigh. "Yes, we can go eat. Seth is here. You will tell him about this, Shelby. No argument."

"As soon as I fill my plate." By now, my stomach thought my throat had been cut and was saying hello to my backbone.

I hurried to the buffet. Oh, grilled chicken, salad, asparagus, and flaky cornbread. I took some of each and went to sit down. "I got tazed while fetching my hat over by where we found the ruby," I said, buttering my bread. "I fell out of the golf cart onto my face. Heath said I had to tell you, so there. I did." I took a bite. Heavenly.

Seth's fork paused halfway to his mouth. A piece of lettuce dropped to his lap. "What?"

"Do I really have to say it again? I'm hungry." I took a bite of parmesan-crusted asparagus.

"When did this happen?"

I thought for a moment. "About two hours ago."

"And you're just now telling me?" He plucked the lettuce from his lap and tossed it on his plate. "Is that why you look like Frankenstein's bride?"

Ouch. I knew I looked bad, but that was a bit over the top. "I've had a really rough day."

"Give her a break, Seth." Cheryl handed him a napkin.

"She worries me. It also bothers me that you want to help her in these escapades."

"I'm a licensed—" I narrowed my eyes.

"PI. Yes, I know." He glanced at Heath who joined us. "Shelby goes nowhere alone."

Again? It seemed as if I was always being assigned a bodyguard.

"Since I'm her partner, I'll be the one," Grandma said. "I've told you before, Shelby, not to leave me behind. Officer Glassman called me again today asking more questions. It's imperative we solve this case…and now."

~

At seven o'clock on the dot, Alice stepped to a podium set up at one end of the diningroom. She banged a gavel on the wood until everyone quieted and she had their attention.

"Ladies and gentlemen." She gripped both sides of the podium. "Once again, Shady Acres has found itself under attack."

Seriously? I glanced at Heath. Was this woman dramatic enough?

"While Betty Jackson may not have been one of us—"

"Good thing," Aggie Harper yelled. "There wouldn't be a man here that was safe."

"Maybe we wouldn't want to be safe from a looker like that," Harold said with a laugh.

Aggie threw a paper cup at his head, splashing those between them with water. "Imbecile!"

"Nag!"

"Please!" Alice banged the gavel again. "What I'm trying to say here is that we need to be vigilant. So, I want to organize a neighborhood watch. Since Betty was murdered in the daylight, we'll need twenty-four surveillance. I've ordered security cameras, but they won't be here for another week. There is a signup sheet at the back of the room. I expect everyone, and I mean every single resident to take a turn. There is enough of us that we won't have to patrol but an hour every few days. Leroy has graciously volunteered to take every night from midnight to one."

Leroy glanced at me and gave a thumbs up.

The door banged in the back of the room as Ted rushed in. He had been suspiciously hard to get a hold of lately. Heath and I still hadn't found the opportunity to question him about his findings.

He caught me looking and gave a nod.

Bingo! He had something for me.

Once the meeting broke up, I dashed for the sign-up sheet to take the hour right after breakfast. That wouldn't interfere with my duties too much and wouldn't be the hottest part of the day. Heath signed up right after I did.

"Ted is waiting for us," he said, his lips near my ear. "Ready?"

"Yes. I thought he would never have time to talk."

We caught up with him, Grandma, Cheryl, and Seth outside Ted's cottage. There was almost an air of gaiety among us. Somehow, I knew Ted had something to say that would lead us further on our quest.

We found seats wherever we could in his sparsely furnished cottage and waited for him to start talking. When several minutes passed, I asked, "What are we waiting for?"

"One more person." Ted peered out the front window. "Ah." He opened the door and let Leroy in, then locked it before turning to us. "I found some information on the internet regarding Bill Millow. It seems he was married quite a few times, each marriage ending as the result of adultery. Now, that doesn't make the man a murderer, but his first wife did die under suspicious circumstances."

I leaned forward on my perch on the sofa's armrest.

"The first Mrs. Millow died in a car accident. The brakes had been cut and the car went over a cliff. I've identified the other two women, both who live here in town. It's the fourth Mrs. Millow that raises a question. Her name was Margaret, but no one seems to be able to locate the woman. This is where Leroy comes in."

Leroy grinned. "As you all know, I wander around at night."

"Snooping," Grandma said. "Call it what it is."

"Okay, snooping. That's a bit of the pot calling the kettle black, but I'll proceed." He glanced at me. "On occasion, Shelby has asked me to keep an extra vigilant attitude on my nightly rounds. I found this." He pulled a folded piece of paper from inside his shirt. "It's a copy of divorce papers of Bill and Sharon Millow. But, Sharon never signed. The divorce hasn't taken place."

"So," Seth said, standing. "I put a call into our lover boy Bill. He's in Europe on an extended leave. If we find Sharon, we might find out who killed Betty. My bet is the latest Mrs. Millow."

"What about driver's license photo?" I raised my hand. "If we knew what she looked like—"

"No driver's license. The woman didn't drive, according to a neighbor. Barely left the house."

"Pictures?" I glanced around the room. "Surely, there are photo albums. A wedding picture?"

"Nothing." Seth shook his head. "Either they never had any or she took them with her when she left. According to the neighbor, the only time Mrs. Millow left the house was to grocery shop and go to the shooting range with her husband. This makes her a dangerous person…if she's our killer."

"How do we find her?" I raised my hand again. "She seems to know what she's doing?"

"Put your hand down," Leroy said. "I also found this." He handed me another piece of paper. "It's a threat letter signed by Mrs Millow. We have a sample of her handwriting."

"And," Ted added, "since we suspect Mrs. Millow is living in Shady Acres under an assumed name, or at least a frequent visitor here, all we need to do is start comparing handwriting."

That was all? That could take weeks, months, years! Still, I might find something in Alice's office. "I'll make copies of that letter and give everyone a copy."

A bullet shattered the front window.

Everyone fell to the floor.

# 12

"Who's shot?" I struggled to get out from under Heath who had wasted no time tackling me to the ground and using his body as a shield.

"Role call!" Seth called out.

"Me," I cried.

Soon, everyone's strong answer rang out. Except for Leroy.

"Let go." I pushed Heath off me and crawled to my friend. "Leroy. Open your eyes for me." I patted his cheek.

His eyelids fluttered. "Ouch."

I ran my gaze over his body, staring in

dismay at the spreading bloodstain on his chest. "Someone call an ambulance."

"Already done," Ted said, pressing a towel against the wound.

Seth unsheathed his weapon and peered out the front window. "Whoever it was is gone."

"Guess…it…doesn't pay…to snoop." Leroy closed his eyes and stopped breathing.

"Help me!" I straddled him and started chest compressions. "Don't you dare die, Leroy. We need you." What would Shady Acres do without one of their most colorful characters?

In the distance, sirens filled the air. Heath and I took turns keeping Leroy's heart beating until two paramedics moved us to the side and took over. They ignored my repeated question as to whether Leroy would live, going about their business with stony expressions.

Shortly after they arrived, so did Officer Glassman. He stood in the doorway and surveyed the room before entering. He headed straight for Seth.

"See anyone?" he asked.

Seth shook his head. "Nope. We were gathered together talking, Leroy was telling us of some information he uncovered, then he was shot."

"You think he was the target?"

"I do. Let's go process the crime scene." With a sad glance at me, he led his partner out of the room.

I started to follow the paramedics before Mom put a hand on my arm to stop me. "I'll ride with him, if they'll let me. You start figuring out who is doing this."

I nodded, then glanced at my blood-smeared hands. I would find this killer. Still staring at my hands, I headed for the bathroom. It took quite a lot of scrubbing before the water ran clear.

"What now?" Heath squeezed in beside me to wash his hands. "The hospital?"

"Not right now. I want to go to Alice's office. There has to be something there."

Bill Millow had a wife and I intended to find her. If Betty was fooling around with him and she found out...well, there was a motive for murder for sure.

"You know Ted isn't going to let you go. He'll say you're breaking and entering."

"But, I'm not." I gave a humorless smile. "I'm getting information for the hoedown this weekend."

He shook his head. "That doesn't make any sense. The fliers have already gone out."

"I need a list of vendors." I marched to my bedroom and retrieved the bag with my gun and Tazer. "Are you coming with me?"

"I'm not letting you go alone."

"Then, let's go." I watched as first reluctance, then resignation flickered across his face. It wasn't fair that I put him in the situation to go with me, but he wouldn't let me go alone. Not if he could help it.

We slipped out the master room

window. The others would discover us gone within minutes, but if we got out of sight, they wouldn't know exactly where we'd gone. I needed all the time I could get before getting caught.

"Shelby, slow down." Heath stepped in front of me. "Do you realize how long it will take to go through all of the files? More time than we have tonight. You're looking for a woman whose name you don't know. It's impossible."

Tears welled in my eyes. "I don't know what else to do."

"Ask for help. The more people looking, the better. We could also go to Millow's house and get fingerprints. Seth said he was out of the country."

"That's illegal." Of course, it was a brilliant idea and I couldn't wait to go. "Don't you think Seth may have already started that process?"

"Most likely, but he won't share the identity if he discovers it. You will. You see things in ways others don't."

"So you're saying wait until morn—" I

caught a glimpse of a flickering light through the window of Alice's office. "Someone beat us here."

He turned, keeping me behind him. "That's a flashlight."

"Which means it isn't Alice." I dug a small penlight from my bag. "Let's go."

"Give me the gun." He held out his hand.

I gladly handed it over. Keeping close to my honey, I let him lead through a back door of the main building. He slipped the lock so the door wouldn't close with a bang and put a finger to his lips.

I nodded and slowly pushed open the door to Alice's office.

Heath entered first, gun held in front of him. "Who's there? I've got a gun!"

"Don't shoot me." Alice aimed the flashlight at her face.

"What in the world are you doing in the dark?" I flipped on the light.

Papers were strewn everywhere. A filing cabinet lay on its side.

"What happened?"

"I came to this after supper. Since I'm smart enough to know someone was looking for something, I left it and came back now. Anyone watching now knows we're here."

I put my hands on my hips. "What were they looking for?"

She bit her bottom lip and ducked her head.

"Alice…"

"I overheard y'all talking about Bill Millow's wife. I've seen that name before. This mess confirms I'm on the right track." She took a deep breath through her nose and stared at me. "I've asked numerous times to be included in your club."

"It isn't a club. I'm a licensed PI. This isn't a game."

"You weren't always licensed."

I rolled my eyes. "Fine. You're in the club." Not that we had one. Grandma insisted we were the Shady Acres Gumshoes, but that was nonsense. "What do you know?"

"That Sharon Millow is living at Shady Acres under an assumed name. I think." She picked up some files from the floor. "Somewhere in this mess is, or was, a paper that listed Sharon Millow as a reference. So, either that person is Sharon or the person knows where Sharon is."

Made sense in a roundabout way. I glanced at Heath.

"It's as good a theory as anything else," he said. "Let's see what we find while we sort this back into order."

Two hours later, I scooted against the wall, legs stretched out in front of me. "Whoever ransacked the office must have found it." My shoulders slumped. Just when we thought we were getting somewhere, something shoved us back. I kicked at an overturned trashcan. An inkpen rolled under the desk.

I crawled after it. The corner of a manilla file folder stuck out from under the area rug. I pulled it free. "Aggie

Harper listed Sharon as her reference. As her only reference," I said holding the file above my head like a trophy.

"I'll take that." Seth entered the office and took the file.

I got to my feet. "Are we going to see Aggie now?"

"I am. You're going home." He motioned his head at Heath, who nodded.

Why did the men around me always work together to thwart my plans?

"Thank you for your help," Seth told us. "But this is police business and Officer Glassman and I will take it from here."

"What about the ruby?"

"I've given it back."

So, it was Glassman's. Poor thing. I really didn't like the man, but I didn't think he was a killer, either. "So, does this clear Grandma?"

"It does make her less of a suspect." He waved for us to leave. "This is now a crime scene."

Alice groaned and stormed ahead of

us. "How am I supposed to work efficiently when my office keeps being off limits?"

"There's an empty desk next to Mom." I grinned.

"Don't be a smart aleck, Shelby. I can't work with the phone ringing all day." She headed one way while Heath and I went the other.

"Don't be too upset," he told me. "We do know something we didn't know before."

"Right." I brightened. "Aggie won't be in her cottage. I'll bet my rainboots she's fled the scene." Which meant…either I'd find her or she'd find me. I wasn't going to stop searching until that happened.

I took Heath's hand. "I'm ready to go see Leroy."

~

Mom sat in the waiting room when we arrived. "He's in surgery. The doctor hasn't come out. The bullet pierced his right lung. The doctor is hopeful, but said surgery would take a while. Leroy started hemorrhaging when they put him in his room. This is his second surgery. You were gone a long time. That's all I know." From the looks of the pile of twisted tissues in her lap, it had been an emotional long time for her.

Hopeful. I'd hold on to that. Good friends were hard to come by, and as weird as he might be, Leroy was a good friend.

Heath went to get us some coffee and something to eat from the vending machine while I filled Mom in on what we discovered in Alice's office.

"She's going to be sitting with me?" She paled.

"There's nowhere else for her to go."

"She could work out of her cottage. It would be quieter and she has a phone."

"You could suggest that." I thought it was a great idea.

I sat back and tried to mentally prepare myself to wait on news of Leroy. I counted ceiling tiles, losing count after two-hundred so I started on floor tiles.

Where was Heath?

I straightened in my chair. How long did it take to get three coffees?

I started to go look for him when the doctor strode toward us. Mom and I met him halfway.

"Mr. Manning is not out of the woods yet, but we believe we were able to stop the bleeding. Not only did the bullet puncture his lung, but it nicked his heart. We'll keep a close eye on him throughout the night. Make sure the receptionist has your phone number for further news." He gave us a small smile, then headed back the way he had come.

Heath ran toward us. "Call Seth. I saw Aggie hanging around Leroy's room. If she's here, then Leroy is in grave danger."

Mom pulled her cell phone from her purse and called Seth. After hanging up, she said, "He's on his way. We need to guard Leroy's room."

"If they'll let us," Heath said. "The doctor ran me off. Said the nurses would keep an eye on him."

"That's not enough." I strained to see down the hall where several people in white coats congregated.

"What room is he in?"

"That one." Heath's eyes widened. "Come on."

At the risk of being run off, we rushed down the hall. "What's happening?" I asked, trying to see into Leroy's room.

"He's fine, Miss. Just a scare." A nurse took me by the shoulders. "His breathing tube fell out. That's all."

Breathing tube? "How could it just fall out?" I turned to Heath. "Aggie's been in his room. Where's the doctor?"

"I'm here." The doctor stepped into the room and closed the door behind him.

Through the small window in the door, I watched as he checked Leroy's vitals, writing them in a chart at the foot of his bed. He exited the room as Seth arrived.

Heath quickly told him of his suspicions.

Seth's features hardened. "I'll guard

the room tonight and send someone else in the morning. We can't let Leroy be her next victim."

# 13

Mom bent over my bed the next morning. "Leroy is awake and asking for you."

I scrambled to my feet and hurriedly pulled on a pair of white capris and a blue sleeveless top. "He survived the night."

"Barely, but he's awake. We'll take each milestone as it comes." She handed me a thermos of coffee and a glazed doughnut. "Heath will meet us in the parking lot."

I slipped my feet into a pair of white flats and rushed out the door.

Mom locked up behind us, at least one

person was thinking straight at seven a.m. Heath leaned against his truck, opening the doors when we arrived. I scooted in first, leaving Mom to sit next to the door. What a blessing the older trucks with their bench seats were.

"Put the pedal to the metal, baby." I grinned up at Heath and offered him a swig from my thermos.

He started the ignition and drove toward the hospital. "No, thanks. I've already had two cups. I'm as excited to see Leroy alive as you are." He squeezed my hand.

"I guess Aggie/Sharon didn't want to try and get past Seth." I bit into my sugary breakfast.

"I guess not." He glanced in his rearview mirror and frowned.

"What?" I looked behind us.

A dark older model truck, a 1985, I thought, rode our bumper. It looked similar to something my father had once owned. Not again. I'd been run off this mountain road more times than I wanted to count. "Speed up, Heath."

"Not so fast that we go over the edge." Mom gripped the dashboard with both hands.

"Relax," I told her. "I know from experience that you don't want to tense up in an accident. You get hurt less if you're relaxed."

Her eyes widened. "Do you realize how crazily like your grandmother you sound right now? How am I supposed to relax when we might run off the road?"

"We don't know that the driver behind us is threatening," Heath said.

The truck rammed us.

"Okay, they're threatening us." Heath pressed the gas pedal. "One of you call Seth."

Ooops. I'd forgotten my bag. We were weaponless. I was a terrible private detective. "You'll have to make the call, Mom."

She peeled one hand off the dashboard and told her phone to call Seth. Cool. She had the app to tell her phone who to call.

"I should get that," I said, as the person behind us hit Heath's truck again.

"Seth! We're on I-85." Mom rattled over the mile marker. "Someone is trying to run us off the road. Hurry." Her phone slid off her lap and onto the floor with another big bump from behind.

Thank the Lord Heath was driving. I would have already lost control.

Our tires squealed as he took a corner sharply. "Hold on," he said. "This is going to get hairy."

Mom screamed as the right tires lifted, then fought again for traction.

The back window shattered.

"They're shooting at us." I pulled Mom down.

Heath scrunched in his seat. "Yep." He spun the wheel. "I will get us out of this. I promise."

I surely hoped it was a promise he could keep. I closed my eyes and prayed. Still, I couldn't help thinking how upset Grandma was going to be when she found out she'd missed the excitement.

Another shot rang out.

"I love you, Heath."

"Ditto, sweetheart, but we aren't going to die." He grunted as another shot rang out.

"Take that road!" Mom pointed to our right.

"I'm not taking us down what could be a deadend."

Finally, we were off the mountain. Ahead of us were the wonderful blinking red and blue lights. Heath stopped in front of them.

I peered out the back window.

The black truck turned a quick U-turn and headed back up the mountain. Coward. A squad car sped after it.

"You did it." I wrapped my arms around Heath.

He groaned.

I glanced down. "You're shot." No, not my honey. "Call an ambulance!" I banged on the window, then started shoving Mom out of the truck. "Tell them to call an ambulance."

"Shelby, stop." Heath put a hand on my arm. "It's a graze. I'm not dying, although I appreciate the dramatics."

"Are you sure?" I studied his face through a veil of tears.

"I'm sure."

Seth appeared at the driver's side window. "Can you drive? If so, we'll make it to the hospital faster than the ambulance can get here and back."

"I can drive."

"I'll have one of the officers take me home," Mom said. "I'm a little shaken up. I'm really not cut out for this kind of stuff."

I smiled. She was tougher than she thought. "I'll see you later. Thank you."

She nodded and stepped back as Heath drove around the parked squad car.

"You're bleeding on your seat." I got on my knees and looked in the small space behind the seat. "Don't you have any clean rags?" The only ones I saw were covered with grease and now shattered glass.

"No need for clean ones." He pulled the truck into a space close to the ER entrance.

I was out of the truck and around to his side before he had the motor shut off. "Lean on me. I can tell you're getting weak."

"Yeah, a little."

We shuffled through the double doors and were immediately escorted to a backroom. I stayed with him while his wound was cleaned and wrapped. Other than a scar to remind him of the morning, he'd be fine, according to the doctor.

"We can visit Leroy in the morning." I smoothed his hair out of his eyes. "You need to get home and rest."

"No, we're already here. Let's go see him."

I agreed, but only if he'd allow me to push him in a wheelchair.

He succumbed and off we went, down hall after hall until we arrived at Leroy's room where Officer Glassman sat in a chair reading a fishing magazine.

"What happened to you?" he asked.

Heath explained our morning. "Leroy asked to see us and we were on our way here when it happened."

Officer Glassman shook his head. "I knew Sharon, briefly, but she didn't strike me as the type to go on a killing spree."

"I don't think she meant to," I said. "I'm sure Betty was her only target until we figured out her identity. She's desperate."

"Desperate people are dangerous." He jerked his thumb toward the door. "Go on in."

"Thanks." I pushed Heath inside.

Leroy gave us a weak smile and raised his bed to a sitting position. "You came. What happened?"

Once again, we explained the morning's events. "I'm so glad to see you breathing."

"Not as glad as I am," he said. "Anyway, I know Seth won't tell you this, but there was a commotion at the nurse's desk last night in an obvious attempt to lure him away from my door. Being the good cop he is, the ruse didn't work. They're transferring me via helicopter this afternoon, but won't tell me where."

"For your protection, I suppose. What do you know that they're protecting?"

"Just what I told you." He shrugged, then grimaced. "I guess Sharon is one pissed off lady and seeking revenge. You need to be careful. Both of you."

"We will." I put a hand on his shoulder. "Take care, Leroy. See you at the wedding."

"Reception. I don't go out until the sun goes down."

"Right." I grinned and wheeled Heath out of the room, relieved that protective measures were being taken to keep my friend alive.

"I need to use the restroom." I parked Heath next to Officer Glassman. "I'll be right back." Despite their protests, I took off.

I shoved through the ladies room door as tremors overtook me. Now that we were safe and Leroy was alive, the dreaded anxiety hit full force. I went into a stall and latched the door closed. If someone were to enter the room and see me they'd think I was having drug withdrawals.

Someone entered a few minutes later and went into the stall next to me. Dread filled me as they stood, silently, not sitting. The hairs on my arms stood on end. I willed my breathing to slow. I needed to get out of there.

Aggie Harper was insanely persistent and willing to take big risks to get her target.

I stood and reached for the stall door.

She did the same.

I yanked mine open and ran out.

She did the same.

I two-hand shoved her into the wall, whirled and sped from the restroom.

Seconds later, I heard the slap of her gym shoes on the tiled floor. "Your nosiness has finally gotten you into real trouble, Shelby Hart."

Nope. Wasn't going to go down this way. I shoved a metal cart at her, grinning at the whoosh of air from her lungs. I raced on until I reached Glassman. "Aggie's here."

He lunged to his feet. "I can't leave this post."

The three of us stared, waiting for her to show herself. Nothing. She was gone. I leaned against the wall. "I never did get to use the restroom."

Glassman stared at me. "Use the one in Leroy's room. Are you insane? If you would have listened when Heath and I told you to stay, you wouldn't have faced her."

"I needed a moment."

The sad look in Heath's eyes told me he understood. I also knew we'd be having a serious conversation about the stress of solving crimes when we got home. Even a kind man like my fiancé had his limits.

Leroy was asleep when I entered his room again. I took care of business, then stepped to the window to close the curtains and shut out the bright sunlight. In the parking lot below, Aggie was stabbing Heath's tires.

I was definitely going to make her pay for all the trouble, one way or the other. I pulled the curtains closed and went to inform Heath he'd have to call a tow-truck.

"I'm going to wring her neck." He furiously punched the buttons on his phone. "It's taken me a long time to restore that truck."

"You can have the retainer Birdie paid me," I offered. "After all, it's because I took this case that your tires were slashed."

"Not a chance." He met my gaze with his serious one. "I was ready to tell you to back off. That this is all too much for you. But now, I'm in full force with you. I want this woman taken down so we can get married and live like normal people."

I wholeheartedly agreed, although I had no idea what normal meant. So many times I'd wanted to stop halfway through my investigations because of the dangers to my family and friends. But every time I realized that I was in too deep and the dangers would come anyway. The only way to make them stop was to take down the killer. Other than Heath and my mother, the others enjoyed the chase much more than I did.

I really needed to rethink this whole PI thing. Maybe I'd do better as a wife and mother with the four bedroom house and a picket fence.

We waited the forty-five minutes the tow-truck said it would take for them to arrive, then said goodbye to Officer Glassman and headed into the afternoon sunlight. I stopped behind a concrete pillar and made sure Aggie was nowhere in the vicinity before wheeling Heath to his truck.

Since the tow-truck driver was a friend of Heath's, he'd replaced the tires for us and we were soon on our way back to Shady Acres.

"We have a police escort this time." Heath glanced in his rearview mirror.

I followed his gaze, relieved to see Seth behind us. It was good to know that even if we butted heads, Seth was going to watch my back.

# 14

It was tough, what with Leroy and Heath getting shot and Heath's truck almost getting run off the road with us in it, but the rented tent for the hoedown looked just like a barn inside. I'd really outdone myself. Thank God for Cheryl's help. If she hadn't gotten the job as receptionist at the police department, I'd have asked Alice to hire her as event coordinator and leave me to the gardening.

Hay bales were scattered around the large area to provide seating. Rough boards lay on the ground as a dance floor.

At one end of the tent was a make-shift stage for the musical instruments and the dance caller. Tables filled with finger foods and drinks sat at the opposite end.

I ran my hands down the pink and blue flouncy skirt and bounced toward my plaid wearing hero. Heath spoke with Bob near the stage and turned to me with a smile.

"I don't think I ever told you I could play the harmonica."

"No, you never did." I clapped my hands. "Will you play tonight?"

"A song just for you." He winked and crooked his arm for me to slide mine through. "Let's eat the refreshments before the piranhas converge."

"An excellent idea."

By the time we filled our sturdy paper plates, Shady Acres residents began filling the tent. Oohs and aahs filled the air. Yep, the hoedown was going to be a hit.

From the corner of my eye, I caught sight of Alice. "Hold this for a second, okay?" I handed Heath my plate and made a beeline for the manager. "Alice, I have an idea."

"Oh, no." She stopped and crossed her arms. "Great job on the tent, by the way."

"That's what I want to talk to you about. Cheryl did it. Now, I'm good at coordinating and decorating, but you have to admit this is stunning. Why not hire her part-time? That would leave me free to focus on the grounds."

"I'm not sure it's in the budget, but I'll talk to corporate." She turned to leave.

"What are you looking for?"

"Seriously, Shelby. Killers always visit crowds when their intended victims will be there. You're obviously a target. I'm keeping an eye out for Aggie." She shook her head and went to stand behind a pillar.

I didn't think I would ever figure that woman out. One minute she acted as if I irritated her, the next she wanted me around for a while. "Well, thanks."

She made a shooing motion with her

hand.

Grinning, I located Heath sitting on a haybale, my plate next to him and his balanced on his knees. "Why is Alice hiding behind that post?" he asked.

"Keeping a look out for Aggie. She's taking her membership in the club seriously." I picked up my plate and sat.

"The more people watching your back, the better." He popped an olive in his mouth. "My shoulder is tender, but I do intend to whirl around this floor with you. Especially with you wearing that short sassy skirt."

"I'm looking forward to it." My face warmed. After almost a year, I still blushed when he got "that" look in his eyes. I hoped he'd look at me that way for the rest of our lives.

The tent soon filled with the sound of fiddles being tuned. My heart raced in excitement. I loved fiddle music and hadn't square danced since high school.

Once the band was ready, the partygoers filled the dance floor. Cheryl looked pleased as punch in her red checkered skirt that matched Seth's shirt. Officer Glassman, in uniform, watched the proceedings from a spot near the door. I guess with Leroy moved, they were no longer needed as protection.

Women faced the men, Bob took his place behind the microphone, a fiddle shrieked…the dancing began. We danced until my feet hurt from the flats I wore and my cheeks felt frozen in a smile. When Heath suggested we take a break and get something to drink, I agreed.

Plastic glasses of punch in hand, we stepped outside the tent for fresh air. I glanced toward the pool in time to see Alice duck through the gate. Strange. I thought she was watching for Aggie from inside.

"Let's go see what that woman—"

A scream cut off my words.

Heath and I threw down our cups and sprinted toward the pool.

Alice pointed at a mannequin lying on one of the pool lounges. Pinned to the mannequin's chest with a knife was a note.

Trembling, I bent for a closer look. Yep, the dark-haired mannequin was supposed to be me. The note had my name scrawled across it and the words 'You're gonna get it now' written in red.

Footsteps pounded and soon Seth, Glassman, and a score of looky-lous crowded the pool area. "Close off the pool," Glassman ordered.

"This woman is like a ghost." Seth glared at the mannequin. "Shady Acres is at full capacity and yet no one sees her running about. Unless—" He turned to study the crowd.

I stepped close to him and whispered, "You think someone is hiding her?"

He nodded. "I can't believe I'm saying this, but can you sneak into the cottages and see if there is something out of the ordinary? Something that doesn't look as if it belongs to the resident?"

"Now?" But I hadn't heard Heath play the harmonica yet.

"As soon as possible."

I was getting tired of people ruining my plans. I pouted, waved for Heath to follow me, and went back to the tent, knowing the residents would soon join us. When the party started again, Heath and I could slip out.

I explained what Seth wanted us to do. "Could you play first?"

"Gladly." He lifted my hand and kissed it then leaped up on the stage.

Soon, a haunting tune that reminded me of trains and loneliness and romance reclaimed filled the tent. Those in attendance stopped what they were doing and swayed in tune as Heath, eyes closed, made magic with the instrument in his hand. If I wasn't already in love with the man that song would do it.

When he finished, he lifted his head and met my gaze with a long smoldering one. Then, he gave a slow wink and jumped to the floor. With a slow, long-legged gait he strolled toward me, took me in his arms, and waved at the band.

The slow melodies of another love song played and we danced while those around us ceased to exist. When the song ended, Heath said, "Now we can do Seth's bidding. I was going to play for you and dance with you no matter what.

Boy I was glad he did. I didn't want to ruin the romance of the evening by digging through other people's lives. Still, I saw the wisdom in looking and while the residents were enjoying the hoedown was our best chance.

"I reckon we should check the women's cottages first," Heath said, steering me from the tent.

At first I'd thought perhaps a man would hide Aggie/Sharon, and that would be a definite if we were looking for the siren, Betty. But Millow's wife…I agreed with Heath. "There's no way we'll get through them all tonight."

"Do you want the cottages first or the apartments?"

"Lorraine might be the type to harbor a fugitive." The wealthy woman who rented the penthouse lived alone and was bored most of the time. I could see her letting Aggie stay with her if only for the excitement.

Heath shuddered. "That woman looks at me as if I'm a slab of beef."

I laughed and patted his shoulder. "You are, sweetie. You're the best eye candy this place has."

He rolled his eyes. "Let's get started before she realizes a down home hoe down isn't a rich city woman's idea of a good time."

He unlocked the main building. "Stairs?"

I nodded. Too many times during an investigation we'd been trapped in the elevator. Not this time.

Pushing open the door, Heath flicked the light switch. Nothing. Nada. Dead. We weren't using the stairs.

# 15

God was smiling on us at that moment. The elevator worked all the way to the penthouse floor.

When the doors opened, Heath peeked out first, then motioned for me to follow him. We hurried to Lorraine's door. Heath knocked three times. When no answer came, he used his master key and let us in, then locked the door behind us. This way, we'd at least get a warning if Lorraine came home early. Or Aggie. I'd like it to be Aggie. I really wanted to put an end to this. My wedding was in less than a month.

Just as the last time we'd snooped in Lorraine's place, it was a mess. What was with her and Grandma cluttering every surface with clothes and makeup. "The hard part is going to be determining whether anything here is not Lorraine's."

Heath nodded, looking stunned as he shined the flashlight I'd had in my bag around the room. "There's…underwear hanging on the lamp."

"That's a slip, honey." I laughed and headed for the bedroom, turning on my penlight.

The only possible idea I could see that might give insight on clothing not Lorraine's would be the quality. The wealthy widow had to be able to afford nicer things than a policeman's wife. I lifted the top item from a stack of clothes on the bed. My hand froze. Right there was the same pea green blouse I'd seen Aggie wear the day Betty was killed.

A lock rattled in the front door.

Heath barged into the bedroom and

grabbed my arm. As he dragged me toward the sliding glass doors to the balcony, I snatched the blouse.

As soon as we closed the curtains and door, the bedroom light switched on. We froze. I'd never been so thankful for black-out curtains before. No one on the inside would see our shadows. We clicked off our lights and pressed our backs against the wall, hopefully out of sight should anyone peer out.

Heath gripped my hand as Lorraine started talking. I turned my head and plastered my eye to a slit in the curtains.

"I don't know why you couldn't just kill Betty and go," she said, removing her dangling earrings. "All you've done now is stir up trouble. Shelby is a Nosy Nelly, but if you'd disappeared as I told you, she wouldn't have discovered your identity."

Nosy Nelly? I clenched my fists. Lorraine had been in on the murder from the beginning.

Aggie entered the bedroom from the living room. "Careful, dear. If she keeps digging, she'll discover we're cousins. How long until she comes knocking on your door with her cop friend."

Lorraine scowled. "You'll be sorry if she does. I'll rat you out. Guarantee it. I was a fool to let you stay here."

"No one thinks to look right under their nose, do they?" Aggie laughed had strolled toward the window.

I managed to duck out of sight right before she yanked open the curtains. Below us, Mom and Grandma were heading home from the hoedown. They glanced up.

I frantically waved them on, hoping, praying Aggie didn't see them.

Mom grabbed Grandma's hand and dragged her off the sidewalk and into the bushes.

"I would have enjoyed the hoedown," Aggie said, turning her back to the window. "It's all that Betty's fault. If she hadn't have messed around with my husband, I—"

"Just stop it." Lorraine sat on the bed

and removed her black stiletto heels. "Everyone in town has been hit on by your husband. A few just happen to take him on it. It doesn't mean anything. If you'd been smart, you'd have divorced him."

Aggie jerked. "You had an affair with my Bill."

"He isn't worth you getting upset about. It was years ago." Lorraine moved to a small vanity and pulled a makeup removed pad from a box.

Aggie bent and picked up one of the stilettos. Before Lorraine could register what was happening in the mirror, Aggie caught her mid-turnaround and buried the stiletto in her temple.

I clapped a hand over my mouth to stifle a squeak. "We have to get out of here," I whispered. "Is the fourth floor to far to jump?"

"Of course, it is." Heath straddled the railing. "Climb on my back. I can make it to the other balcony. We'll knock. If no one lets us in, we'll keep heading down until someone does or we reach the bottom."

"Your legs won't reach. You're crazy!"

"We don't have a choice, Shelby. Get on my back!" He grabbed my arm and pulled me closer.

"Can't I just shoot her? I have my gun. Let me shoot her."

"Hey!" Ted yelled up at us. "What in tarnation are you two doing now?"

His yell caught Aggie's attention because she appeared at the window. She glanced down at him, his eyes widened, then she turned her attention to us.

I read the curse word on her lips and scrambled onto Heath's back when she ducked back. "Hurry."

Aggie returned seconds later with a gun. She slid the door open.

Before she could fire on us, Ted fired. He missed, chipping off a chunk of stuccoinstead of hitting her.

Aggie jumped back.

"I'll try to head her off." Ted dashed

for the door to the apartments.

"You'll need a key," Heath called out. "It's in my pocket."

No way either of us could retrieve it hanging on the side of the building like we were. Heath jumped, grabbing the next railing. Our bodies slammed against the iron bars. My breath left my body in a whoosh.

"You okay?" Heath grunted.

"Yes, you?"

"Hit my side. We'll worry about that when we get down."

"Get in here." The door on the other side of the patio opened and Dean Roof, wearing plain pajamas, called out.

We couldn't scramble over fast enough. Heath stopped and tossed Ted the keys, then shoved me inside the apartment. "Thanks, Dean," he said.

"Good thing I didn't go to the function. This cold has kicked my rear. Want a beer?" Dean raised his eyebrows.

"No, thanks. Is your door locked?" Heath answered.

"Yes, why—"

Someone banged on the door.

Dean moved toward it.

"No!" Heath and I yelled in unison. Great. If it was Aggie, we'd just told her for sure where we were.

"It's Ted! Let me in! Have your gun ready. Hurry."

Heath leaped forward and yanked open the door while I pulled my gun from my purse.

Ted fell inside, bleeding heavily from his arm. "That psycho jumped out and shot me. No idea where she is now. I barely got away with my life."

Heath slammed and locked the door. "We saw her kill Lorraine. Aggie was staying there. She killed Lorraine, who happens to be her cousin, when Lorraine said something about an affair with Bill. She really is out of her mind."

My legs would no longer support me and I fell onto Dean's leather couch while Heath tied a dishtowel around Ted's arm. Killed with a shoe! An expensive shoe, but right to the head. I covered my face with my hands until I realized Aggie was still out there. I dug my phone from my bag and called Seth, noticing Heath's shoulder was bleeding.

"You're bleeding," I said.

"What?" Seth barked.

"Not you, Heath."

"What are you talking about, Shelby?"

"We found Aggie. She killed Lorraine and stabbed Ted. We're locked in a third-floor apartment with Dean Roof."

"How bad is Ted hurt? Heath?"

"Heath's is the bullet graze. He banged in while jumping from one balcony to another with me on his back. I'm no doctor, but I think they both need medical attention. Plus, Aggie is still around here somewhere. She's got a gun."

"I'm on my way. Stay put." Click.

I called Mom, explained the situation, and told her to get Grandma and lock themselves in one of their cottages. I could hear Grandma calling Ted's name in the background. "Tell her, he's fine," I said. "We'll come to you later."

"We're going to Bob's. Be careful, Shelby." Mom hung up.

Two hours later, Seth and Officer Glassman arrived and woke me up. I wiped drool from my cheek and sat up, my face flaming. Who in their right mind falls asleep when hiding from a killer?

Heath got my look and grinned. "You needed it."

"I guess."

"She's gone," Seth said. "Not a trace except for Ted's blood in the hall and Lorraine's body in her apartment. What a way to go. Let's get you two to a hospital. Ted probably needs stitches."

"My bleeding has stopped," Heath said. "I'd rather take Shelby home. Ida and Sue Ellen are waiting for news."

"I'll take Ted, if you want to escort them," Officer Glassman told Seth. "I don't think any of this group should be without protection."

"I agree." Seth motioned his head to the door. "Let's go, folks. Keep your eyes open. Just because we didn't find her, doesn't mean she isn't around. The woman's elusive."

We walked through a moonless night toward Bob Satchett's cottage. No one spoke.

I searched the foliage, expecting Aggie to leap out with a banshee shriek. Which would put me right into a heart attack. I grabbed Heath's good arm and pressed close to his side.

He put his arm around me. "We'll be fine."

"In all the investigations I've gotten involved in, none have been like her." Sure, I'd been chased through the maze, the underground tunnels, the forest, but this was a game of cat and mice. I knew where the other people who had wanted me dead had been. Aggie flitted in and out like a murderous shadow.

Bob answered Seth's knock and ushered us inside.

"How's my Teddy?" Grandma clutched Seth by the shoulders. "I'm going to kill that woman when I find her."

"You'll stay out of it." Seth removed her hands. "She's too dangerous. I'm sorry I asked Shelby to look around." He shook his head. "You two could have been killed. I couldn't have lived with that." He glanced up. "Where's Cheryl?"

# 16

How could I not have noticed my Amazon best friend wasn't with us? "Heath and I were a bit preoccupied," I said. "Wasn't she with y'all?"

Mom and Grandma glanced at each other, then Mom said, "She was, until she had to go to the restroom." She glanced at her watch. "That was quite a while ago, come to think of it."

"Do you think Aggie got her?" Grandma's eyes widened. "I think it would be hard for someone small like Aggie to take down Cheryl."

I agreed, except Aggie had a gun. "If Aggie did take Cheryl from the dance, where could she have gone? We just saw her in Lorraine's apartment until she ran. The first place to check is the bathroom." I reached for the handle on the front door.

"Not alone." Seth stopped me. "I'll go with you. It isn't safe. Ida, give Heath your gun. We'll be back as soon as we can."

He peered out, then slowly opened the door. He obviously expected Aggie to be in wait, gun in hand.

"We could go out the back," I suggested.

"She could be there as easily as here." He stepped out. When nothing happened, he waved me to join him.

Not wanting to put myself at more risk, I increased my speed until I was practically running. A fast moving target is harder to hit, right? Upon reaching the diningroom, I slammed through the door. Once Seth was inside, I plastered, my back to it and fought to regain my breath.

The diningroom was dark. No light shined from under the swinging kitchen doors. Somewhere in the recesses of the building a clock chimed midnight. I shuddered.

"Come on." Seth flicked on a small flashlight and, keeping the beam focused on the ground, led me down the short hall. He reached for the women's restroom door.

"You can't go in there."

He glanced over his shoulder. "Seriously? The only person that might be in there is Cheryl or Aggie. I doubt I'm going to see anything I shouldn't." He shook his head and entered the room.

I was as close behind him as I could be without riding piggyback.

"Cheryl?" I whispered.

A thumping noise came from the handicap stall.

Seth rushed forward and yanked open the door.

Gagged and tied to the toilet was a very irate Cheryl.

"What happened?" Seth asked, cutting away the duct tape that kept her hands around the plumbing.

I untied the headscarf from around her mouth.

"Aggie hit me just as I entered the stall. Get out. My bladder is going to burst!"

Seth scurried backward.

I laughed and leaned against the sinks. "You didn't see her?"

"I heard something and turned just as I was getting ready to close the stall door. She hit me with something. That's all I know." She sighed loudly. "Is Seth still in here?"

"I'm here."

"Leave please. I can't go while you're in here."

"For crying out loud." He stormed from the restroom.

Cheryl promptly released her bladder. "I wasn't out long because I could feel the torture of having to go the bathroom."

The sound of moving clothing reached

my ears, then the door opened and she headed for the sinks.

"I wonder why she didn't kill me?"

"You're lucky. She stabbed Lorraine Harding in the temple with a stiletto. I know, because Heath and I were on the balcony and I saw the whole thing."

"There's a story there."

"It'll have to wait until we get back. If Seth waits too long, he'll be in a bad mood."

Seth backed into the room before we could leave. "Shh. We aren't alone."

Cheryl clutched me like a lifeline. I wiggled free so she wouldn't crush me. "Aggie?" I whispered.

"Probably."

The three of us crowded into the handicap stall, the one we'd found Cheryl in. Seth slowly closed the door, leaving just enough of a crack for him to peer out of.

"Do you think she's coming back to finish me off?' Cheryl asked, clutching me again.

"I don't know."

The light came on, blinding me.

Seth leaped out. "Hands up!"

Somebody screamed.

When I could see again, I looked out to see Joyce with her hands over her head. "I thought y'all left."

"I'm the only one here. I had to do an inventory of the pantry." She cocked her head. "Can I put my hands down?"

Seth nodded.

"We didn't see any lights on," I said.

"I only had the light on in the pantry. You know how big that room is. I still have at least an hour's worth of work and morning comes early. May I do what I came for and leave?" Her eyes narrowed. "Why is there a man in here with you?"

"Police business." Seth marched past her.

Cheryl and I followed him back to Bob's cottage.

The other four leaped to their feet when we walked in.

"I'll get you a cup of coffee," Mom

said, heading for the kitchen."

"Where were you?" Grandma looked up from the sofa, a glass of wine in her hand.

"The bathroom." Cheryl plopped onto the sofa. "Where's Ted?"

Tears welled in Grandma's eyes. "He was shot. I'm waiting on news while I drown my fears."

Seth pulled his cell phone from his pocket, dialed a number, and moved down the hall. He returned a few minutes later. "Ted is out of surgery and doing fine. You can go see him now."

She set her glass on the coffee table. "Will you take me?"

He nodded. "Just as soon as everyone is safely ensconced in their cottages."

Bob, who had remained silent, stood from his leather easy chair. "I really had no idea what I was getting into dating Sue Ellen. Sure, I knew what a loose cannon Shelby was. That's part of her charm. But, whooee, this is almost more excitement than this old man can take."

"Oh, hush, and have another cup of coffee." Mom handed him a cup, then turned to Cheryl. "I guess this means you won't have time to drink a cup."

Cheryl shrugged and slipped her arm through Seth's. "I am tired."

"Come on, Mom. You're staying with me tonight. Heath, can you stand sleeping on the sofa?"

He grinned. "If it helps keep you safe, I can sleep on the floor."

*Sweet man. I just want everyone under one roof, if possible.*

~

The sun dawned bright and clear the next morning with no sign of Aggie. Her car was no longer in the parking lot. Once again, she'd snuck in and out under Seth's nose and he was furious. It didn't help that Glassman kept telling him at breakfast that it would take more than one man to catch the woman.

"She's a ghost, I tell you. She's been trained by the best." He pointed a strip of bacon at Seth. "Millow is a good cop.

Maybe not a morally upstanding man, but he knows his job. Some of it had to have rubbed off on his wife."

"Shut up." Seth shoved a forkful of ham and cheese omelet into his mouth.

"Why hasn't anyone called Millow?" I glanced around the table. "I know he's out of the country, but is he out of reachability, too?"

Glassman tossed down his napkin. "Millow is dead, girlie. Found in the trunk of his car this morning. Been dead for weeks. My guess is his wife offed him before taking out that Betty lady. A neighbor smelled him when she was doing yard work near his garage. What a way to go."

I shoved my plate away.

"She isn't a ghost," Heath said. "She's around here somewhere. If Shelby is her next target, she isn't going to go far."

I didn't like that thought at all. "The tunnels?"

Seth shook his head. "Already looked."

"Maze? The woods?"

"Checked the maze. We'll need more men to check the woods. The FBI is coming in this afternoon. Sharon Millow is officially a serial killer now."

More like a wife that had gone insane, but they could call her whatever they wanted. I had a wedding creeping ever closer and needed this solved. Like now.

"Ah." Glassman straightened in his chair. "The feds are here early." He stood and went to greet them. Within seconds, he'd glanced at Seth, who then went to join them, and the four left.

"If she isn't in the…" I thought of a vacant building I'd once seen near the lake. A boathouse, no longer used. "I think I know where Aggie is."

"Let's go." Heath looped my bag over his shoulder. "We're loaded. Text Seth and tell him where we're headed. Where are we headed?"

"The old boathouse."

He grinned. "Smart gal."

Once again, Grandma was going to be

upset. But her and Mom had elected to stay at the hospital with Ted. It was for the best. The less people tromping toward the boathouse, the easier it would be to sneak up.

"Ready?"

"Ready."

"Where are we going?" Alice jumped in front of us. "I found out something."

"You did? What?"

"Aggie/Sharon's family owns a little house on the other side of the lake. This lake used to be quite the vacation getaway, until the corporation we work for bought up all the land and built this community. Except…they couldn't get Sharon's family to sell. I'll tell you exactly where it is if you let me go with you."

I glanced at Heath.

He nodded. "I'll get the four-seat cart."

Alice and I followed him to the storage shed. My nerves tingled. Within half an hour, I might come face-to-face, once again, with a killer.

# 17

"See?" Alice said, sliding into the front passenger seat. "I'm good at this. You should have let me join a long time ago."

I would have eventually stumbled across the information. If she had hidden it in her office, it was only a matter of time. I crossed my arms and glared at the back of her head. Then, I remembered I was to text Seth and tell him where we were headed. So I did, then resumed my glaring while Alice chatted it up with Heath.

I allowed myself a good sulk, then

concentrated on the task ahead. My bag sat on the seat next to me and held my investigating tools. My gun, my Tazer, a flashlight, a pad of paper and pencil. My cellphone possessed a high resolution camera. I felt ready for whatever awaited us.

Leaning forward, I put my hand on Heath's shoulder. "We could end this today. Then, there's nothing ahead of us but our wedding."

He put his hand over mine. "Let's hope so."

"Gag." Alice turned her head. "Take the east path. It's rough and bumpy, but she won't see us coming."

A good thing since she was such a good shot. "Should we wait for Seth?"

"We will," Heath said. "Unless we spot Sharon, we stay in the cart until the authorities arrive."

"But, shouldn't we check to make sure she's been there?" Alice frowned. "You know the police are going to make us go back."

"Shelby and I have already been chased by this crazy woman. I'm not looking forward to it happening again." Heath's shoulders tensed even though his kept his voice calm.

We rode in silence until the cabin came into view. Then, Alice clutched the dashboard. "Stop here."

We peered through the cart's front window. The small cabin seemed unassuming and vacant. I didn't expect smoke to spiral from the chimney since it was early summer, but it was the barely hanging onto the frame front door that led me to believe no one was there.

"Has Seth answered?" Heath leaned forward, his gaze glued to our surroundings.

"No."

"Then, I'm not waiting." Alice slid from the golf cart and was off before Heath could reach over and grab her.

"Idiot," he muttered.

"Here's the gun." I knew without asking that we were going after her.

"Stay behind me."

I nodded, dug the Tazer from my bag, then slung the bag over my shoulder and followed Heath toward the cabin. I was going to help Heath kill Alice when we got home. I'd made some bonehead moves in my time, but when you have a woman as fleeting and good at killing as Sharon, a person needed to be more cautious.

Alice ducked under a window, her hands clutching the sill, eyes wide. She waved us forward without taking her eyes off whatever was inside.

Heath and I bent over and rushed to her side. "What is it?" I asked.

"She's definitely been here, or at least someone has, but they aren't here now. Let's go in." She slid sideways and squeezed through the opening left by the hanging door.

Heath growled and took my hand. "I'm going to strangle her."

"I'll help you." Staying behind Heath, we moved closer toward the door.

My phone went off.

A shot rang out.

A thud sounded inside the house, then pounding feet and the slamming of a door.

Heath and I glanced at each other, then peered around the doorframe.

Alice lay on the floor in a puddle of blood. She wasn't moving. I suddenly felt terrible about my earlier thoughts toward killing her. "Is she dead?"

Heath shrugged. "Stay back." He grabbed a chunk of firewood from a pile on the porch and tossed it into the cabin. When no one fired at it, we crept inside.

I checked Alice's neck for a pulse. Nothing. The single gunshot had gone through her heart.

My knees weakened and I folded to the dusty floor. Alice and I might not have been the best of friends, in fact she often got on my nerves, but I couldn't imagine Shady Acres without her.

I sniffed and wiped the tears from my eyes. "She's gone."

Heath heaved a sigh. "It looks like Sharon got away again. We can't stay here. She might come back."

"What about Alice? We can't leave her."

He glanced at her body. "What's the protocol here? It's a crime scene now. Are we allowed to move her?"

"Better to ask forgiveness later."

He nodded and lifted Alice into his arms. "Let's go. Quick."

We ran across the lawn, me repeatedly looking over my shoulder. Heath laid Alice on the backseat as I climbed into the front. Once he was in the driver's seat, we turned around and raced down the bumpy path toward home…and safety.

We met Seth and Officer Glassman halfway there. We didn't stop, instead leaving them to follow. Their eyes widened at the sight of Alice in the backseat, but ncither one said anything until we stopped.

"What happened?" Seth asked.

"She barged into the cabin where Sharon was hiding," Heath said, plucking his bloody shirt away from his body. "She was shot. At least we think it was Sharon. Alice is the only one who might know for sure, and she can't tell us."

"You shouldn't have disturbed the scene," Glassman said.

"I suspect as much, but she's one of us. We couldn't leave her."

"We'll need a statement."

"Yes, sir, as soon as I changed out of this shirt and clean off her blood. I'll meet you at Shelby's cottage." Without a backward glance, Heath marched away.

Sorrow showed in the line of his slumped shoulders. Still, I knew my man would do what needed doing, and if he needed to mourn, he'd do it at a later time. I blinked away more threatening tears and waited with the two police officers for the ambulance.

I wanted something to use to cover Alice. Something to keep her out of sight before anyone in the community saw her.

It would be supper soon and once the bell rang, the entire community would traipse past, if not before. In the distance, sirens rang out. Hopefully, the residents were used to the sound from past escapades of mine.

Two paramedics carried a board to us and gently placed Alice on it. I couldn't stop the tears then. They flowed freely as they carried her away.

Seth put his arm around me. "Come on, Shelby. Let's get your statement, then Officer Glassman and I will head to the cabin."

"She's gone." Was I speaking of Alice or Sharon?

"We'll eventually catch her. As long as she keeps coming, she'll make it easier and easier."

I jerked away. "Every time she comes, somebody dies!" I two-hand shoved him. "Why haven't you caught her yet? You're a cop!"

Officer Glassman held my arms behind me. "Settle down, girlie. You're assaulting a police officer."

"Let her go," Seth said. "I'm a friend right now, not an officer. Shelby, we're trying. I'm sorry about Alice, really I am. Sharon is always one step ahead of us. But she will mess up."

I sniffed. "Not soon enough." I stormed away from them to my cottage, locking the door before they could enter. Heath had a key so he'd let them in when he arrived, but for now…they could leave me alone.

I plopped onto the sofa and placed my arm over my eyes. Stupid license. I didn't want to be a private investigator anymore. I wanted the perfect life. The house and picket fence life. I had the perfect man already. The rest would fall into place if I could just leave the allure of danger alone.

Seriously, it was an illness. Well, no more. I was going to marry Heath and say no to anymore requests to solve a crime. Shady Acres had to be cursed! How many times could a killer reside within the community anyway?

Or was it just that I was unlucky? First, Donald ditches me at the altar, literally. Then, I find the job at Shady Acres and a dead body almost immediately. The deaths hadn't stopped since. I almost wanted to ask whether the community had been built on a burial ground and forever doomed.

# 18

A week after Alice's somber memorial, since the police had yet to release her body, my wedding day dawned.

I stood in my just-above-the-knee scalloped hem wedding dress and peered through the lace curtains over the window of Mom's cottage. Mom, the new manager of Shady Acres. I shook my head. She continued to surprise me, but not as much as Grandma temporarily taking over the job of receptionist.

"You look very pretty." Grandma wrapped her arms around me from behind. "Even though that isn't the dress I would have chosen for you."

I smiled at the gauzy, breezy dress Grandma wore. Not white, but a pale yellow that went with her Lucille Ball dyed red hair. "You look beautiful."

"Oh, go on with you." She waved a hand. "Our ride will be here soon. Are you ready?"

I nodded. Bob was picking us up in the golf cart and giving us a ride to the maze. Not the wedding I'd wanted by the lake, but with Aggie/Sharon still on the loose, Seth thought we'd be safer here. At least he hadn't asked us to postpone the day.

"You both look very lovely." Mom said, entering the room. Her eyes shimmered. "I'm so happy for you, Shelby. You, too, Mom."

I grinned. "Tell me Heath is waiting for me."

"That man is as nervous as a possum under a floodlight. This one isn't going to ditch you. Bob texted and said he'd be here in five minutes."

"I'd better visit the little girl's room." Grandma lifted the hem of her long gown and fluttered out of the room.

"I'll go watch for him and give a holler when he's here." Mom cupped my cheek. "You look very beautiful."

"I feel beautiful."

She blinked away tears and left me to wait.

I grabbed my tube of lip gloss from a small side table and leaned close to the mirror to apply it. Once my lips were rosy, I smacked them together and straightened, sliding my hand over my cell phone, and looked up right into the barrel of Sharon's gun. I slipped the phone into the bra cup of my dress, pressing the on button as I did so. "You aren't invited to my wedding."

"Well, don't you look nice." She poked the barrel into my spine. "You'll look very pretty when they bury you. Nice and quiet, now. Out the back door."

This could not be happening. My second attempt at getting married was being thwarted. I'd strangle Aggie at the first opportunity, and wrong or not, I'd enjoy it immensely. I reached for my bag.

"Nope. You won't need that."

Ugh. I marched out the back on my high heels. A rusty rat-trap of a Dodge truck, at least twenty years old, waited idling.

"Get in." She jabbed me again.

I got in. Seconds later, we were roaring across the grounds of Shady Acres and right past my beloved fiancé.

He took one look and sprinted for his truck. Good man. My hero would follow and save the day. But, I still hoped I could at least punch Aggie for disrupting the day before she was hauled away. "Where are we going?"

"Don't worry. It's a beautiful place. Wouldn't want to kill you on your wedding day in an ugly spot."

"You're crazy. You really are." I turned in my seat. "You aren't the only woman in the world to get cheated on, you know. My former fiancé cheated multiple times. I didn't go around killing people."

"To each their own." She whipped the steering wheel to the left, careening past a car in the next lane, and taking us down a dirt road.

We were going to the lake. I sighed. The place I originally wanted my wedding. "Are we going to the cabin?" I hoped not. I didn't want to go back to the place Alice had died.

"Don't be silly. The cops will look for us there. I know of a much better place. There's a lovely little meadow."

"Why me? I didn't have anything to do with your husband. In fact, I've never met him. You either, until you moved to Shady Acres. Why did you move here?"

"Lorraine suggested I come. As for you…well, you got in the way." She cut me a sideways glance. "You're too smart for your own good, Shelby. I like you. We could have been friends. I might have hired you someday."

Not likely. How badly did I want to get

away? Very much. I ran my hands down my beautiful dress, then grabbed the door handle, shoved open the door…and jumped. I rolled down an embankment. No time to catch the breath I'd knocked from my lungs. I removed my heels and carried them with me into the woods.

The hairstyle Mom had labored over came loose and hung in my eyes. Mud covered the once white fabric of my wedding gown. I'd wear overalls to my next wedding. Heath wouldn't mind. He'd be so happy to see me alive that he'd let me wear my gardening boots.

"Shelby Hart, I'm going to shoot you down!" Sharon's voice rang out.

I glanced behind me. Where was she? I hunkered down behind a thick bunch of bushes and pulled out my cell phone. The screen was cracked from my leap out of the truck, but still working. That meant as long as I had a signal, Heath could track me.

I groaned at my skinned knees, then pushed back to my feet. A thick branch leaned against a rock. I gripped it with both hands and waited.

"When did you figure out it was me?" Sharon's voice came from somewhere to my right. "I know you found out before I killed my cheating cousin. Did that stupid Alice help you? I know she was nosing around. Or was it that handsome cop? Oh, well. It doesn't matter now. You're the one I want. Then…I'll shoot the cop. Maybe your fiancé after that. I mean, why not? I'm on a spree. Once I'm caught I'm going to jail for a very long time."

A twig snapped. "Oh, I bet is was dear Teddy. I like him. He couldn't be swayed by Betty's charms. I'll let him live."

Oh, goody. The woman was definitely a crayon short of a full box.

Sharon strolled toward me as if she didn't have a care in the world. In fact, she whistled the jaunty tune, "Whistle while you work", from the movie Snow White.

I gripped my weapon tighter, waiting, waiting…there. I jumped up and swung.

"That's for ruining my dress!" The stick caught her in the shoulder, knocking the gun from her hands. "This is for Alice." I whacked her in the head, bringing her to her knees.

I dropped the stick and twisted one hand in her hair while the other grabbed her dropped pistol. "Now, you get up." I yanked.

"Ow!" She put her hands over mine. "That hurts."

"Not as much as I want it to." Keeping one hand tight on her hair and the other one holding the gun, I half-dragged, half-pushed the larger woman back the way we'd come.

"Are you off your meds, Sharon?" I asked. "Because no one acts like you unless they're psychotic. Seriously? You run around half-cocked, killing anyone who crosses you."

"I found it fun. Ow! Stop yanking my head around!"

God forgive me, but I was actually enjoying myself. "Stop whining. You were going to kill me."

I stopped at the foot of the embankment. There was no way I could drag her up there. I'd need both hands just for myself. "Sit." I pulled her down. "We'll wait here."

We didn't have to wait long. Soon the road above us was crowded with vehicles containing Heath, Bob, Ted, Seth, and Officer Glassman. They stood above us staring down.

Heath smiled at the sight of me pulling Sharon's hair. "Let's get married, Shelby."

"Can we lock her up somewhere first?"

Seth and Glassman slid down the embankment. "We'll cuff her and put her in the squad car. Let go."

"I can't. It's kind of tangled." And cutting off my circulation, but I wasn't going to complain. I was still alive and breathing.

"Use this." Glassman grinned and handed Seth a pocketknife. "She doesn't need to look pretty where she's going."

Seth laughed and hacked away until Sharon's blond hair fell at our feet and I was free.

"My hair!" Sharon kicked Seth in the shin.

Glassman grabbed her and cuffed her. "Now, unless you want us to give you back to Shelby, I suggest you find a way to get your sorry butt up that hill."

Sharon cursed and turned around. Using her feet as leverage, she pushed and grunted until she was close enough for Ted to grab her. Moments later, she was cursing and screaming in the backseat of Glassman's car.

A horn honked. I turned to see Mom and Grandma drive up and stop next to us. "I'm married!" Grandma shouted. "We couldn't wait. We thought you skipped out."

"No, we didn't." Mom cut the ignition. "Heath told us what happened. Mom and Ted said quick vows in case Ted got killed saving you."

I laughed and went to Heath.

He wrapped his arms around me. "Let's get married."

Bob pulled a little black book from inside his suit jacket. "I've got my license."

"Here?" I peered into Heath's face. "Look at me. I'm muddy, bleeding, my hair—"

He lowered his face and kissed me. "You've never looked more beautiful to me."

"I lost my shoes back there somewhere…I don't have a bouquet…"

"Please. Don't make me live another day without being your husband." He strode to the water's edge and pulled up a handful of wildflowers, holding them out to me.

Tears rolled down my face as I took them. "Alright, Heath. I'll marry you. Right now. There on the shore of the lake, just as we'd planned."

Holding hands, we stepped to the water's edge.

Bob opened his book. "Dearly beloved…"

## The End

Dear Reader,

I hope you've enjoyed the six Shady Acres adventures with Shelby's family and friends. Sadly, their tale is complete. Stay tuned for my new series…Paparazzi mysteries. While you wait, peruse the following list. You're sure to find something you like.

God bless,
Cynthia Hickey

Enjoy other books by Cynthia Hickey

## Shady Acres Mysteries
Beware the Orchids, book 1
Path to Nowhere
Poison Foliage
Poinsettia Madness
Deadly Greenhouse Gases

## INSPIRATIONAL
(scroll down to see clean books without

inspirational message)

Nosy Neighbor Series
Anything For A Mystery, Book 1
A Killer Plot, Book 2
Skin Care Can Be Murder, Book 3
Death By Baking, Book 4
Jogging Is Bad For Your Health, Book 5
Poison Bubbles, Book 6
A Good Party Can Kill You, Book 7 (Final)
Nosy Neighbor collection

Christmas with Stormi Nelson

The Summer Meadows Series
Fudge-Laced Felonies, Book 1
Candy-Coated Secrets, Book 2
Chocolate-Covered Crime, Book 3
Maui Macadamia Madness, Book 4
All four novels in one collection

The River Valley Mystery Series
Deadly Neighbors, Book 1
Advance Notice, Book 2

## The Librarian's Last Chapter, Book 3
### All three novels in one collection

### Historical cozy
### Hazel's Quest

### Historical Romances
### Runaway Sue
### Taming the Sheriff
### Sweet Apple Blossom

### Finding Love the Harvey Girl Way
### Cooking With Love
### Guiding With Love
### Serving With Love
### Warring With Love
### All 4 in 1

### A Wild Horse Pass Novel
### They Call Her Mrs. Sheriff, book 1 (A Western Romance)

### Finding Love in Disaster

The Rancher's Dilemma
The Teacher's Rescue
The Soldier's Redemption

## Woman of courage Series

A Love For Delicious
Ruth's Redemption
Charity's Gold Rush
Mountain Redemption
Woman of Courage series (all four books)

## Short Story Westerns
Desert Rose
Desert Lilly
Desert Belle
Desert Daisy
Flowers of the Desert 4 in 1

## **Romantic Suspense**

## Overcoming Evil series
Mistaken Assassin
Captured Innocence

Mountain of Fear
Exposure at Sea
A Secret to Die for
Collision Course
Romantic Suspense of 5 books in 1

The Game
Suspicious Minds

**Contemporary**

Romance in Paradise
Maui Magic
Sunset Kisses
Deep Sea Love
3 in 1

Finding a Way Home

Service of Love

**Christmas**

Handcarved Christmas
The Payback Bride

<u>Curtain Calls and Christmas Wishes</u>
<u>Christmas Gold</u>
<u>A Christmas Stamp</u>

## The Red Hat's Club (Contemporary novellas)

<u>Finally</u>
<u>Suddenly</u>
<u>Surprisingly</u>
<u>The</u> Red Hat's Club 3 – in 1

## CLEAN BUT GRITTY

Colors of Evil Series

<u>Shades of Crimson</u>

The Pretty Must Die Series

<u>Ripped in Red, book 1</u>
<u>Pierced in Pink, book 2</u>
<u>Wounded in White, book 3</u>
<u>Worthy, The Complete Story</u>

## Lisa Paxton Mystery Series

### Eenie Meenie Miny Mo
### Jack Be Nimble
### Hickory Dickory Dock

### One Hour (A short story thriller)

Made in United States
North Haven, CT
04 July 2023